AGAINST THE ODDS

BOOK 1 IN THE FROBISHER FAMILY SAGA

KAY RACE

Copyright © October 2021 by Kay Race

All rights reserved.

No part of this book may be reproduced in any form or by any electronic or mechanical means, including information storage and retrieval systems, without written permission from the author, except for the use of brief quotations in a book review.

Cover design by Jim Divine, copyright November 2021

All characters and events portrayed in this novel, other than recognisable historical ones, are fictitious and any similarity to actual people or events is coincidental.

❀ Created with Vellum

For Keith, my rock, the love and light of my life.

*In loving memory
of
Deborah Goodall*

26th November 1965 - 5th June 2017

Hippocratic oath:

— "First, do no harm"

CONTENTS

Foreword	xi
Main Characters	xiii
1. 4 Hatton Place	1
2. Letty	9
3. The matriculation examination and vilification	18
4. Hope, then hope dashed	28
5. The aftermath	37
6. The Meeting at Lauder Road	46
7. Charles finds a solution	51
8. The Edinburgh Six	59
9. That afternoon	64
10. Saturday, 4th June	70
11. Edinburgh Royal Infirmary	79
12. Later that morning	85
13. Red Letter Day	91
14. Funding strategy Meeting	97
15. Putting "fun" into fundraising	101
16. The Scotsman to the rescue	106
17. Saturday, 30th July 1887	111
18. An unexpected outcome	116
19. The Journey Begins	121
20. Letters from Letty	127
21. December 1887	131
22. Christmas Day 1887	137
23. More Letters ...	145
24. Perils of the Dublin Slums	151
25. Letty is admitted to hospital	158
26. Louisa parts company with The Edinburgh Children's Refuge	163
27. Edinburgh School Board, monthly meeting	168
28. Letters from Letty	174

29. 4 Hatton Place ... 178
30. Incident on the Forth Bridge ... 183
31. Louisa agrees to see Rose ... 192
32. Later that day ... 197
33. Rose meets Louisa ... 201
34. The Edinburgh Six ... 207
35. Graduation ... 216
36. The return of the Edinburgh Six ... 220
37. In conclusion ... 226

Afterword ... 231
Acknowledgments ... 235
About the Author ... 237
Also by Kay Race ... 239
Glossary of Scots Words ... 241
Miscellaneous Notes ... 243

FOREWORD

People here in the UK, in the second decade of the 21st century, may find it difficult to imagine what life was like in the late Victorian era when there was no: electricity; motor powered vehicles; telephones; smart phones; computers; X-Rays; MRI and CT scans; blood transfusions; a National Health Service etc. etc. The list could go on and on, but this is sufficient to demonstrate what a different world we are living in now.

We take so many things for granted today. One of which is that women have access to higher education and have the opportunity to do many degrees that were, at one time, the jealously-guarded domain of males. Studying for and attaining a medical degree is a good example. Then, women were not allowed to study at degree level in many universities and there was strong and, at times, violent opposition to women training as doctors. The doors of medical schools up and down the country had been firmly closed to them. In the occasional instances when women had been given permission to study medicine, the subsequent opposition and trouble, caused by male students, resulted in universities rescinding that permission.

This happened in Edinburgh in 1870, when seven women were attacked, physically and verbally, by a mob of male students, while trying to gain entry to their anatomy exam. The women were called *The Edinburgh Seven* and they had to go abroad to complete their medical training. The incident was called the *Surgeon's Hall Riot* and was widely covered in the newspapers of the day.

Interestingly, and very belatedly in 2019, (almost one hundred and fifty years later) the Edinburgh Medical School awarded the seven women posthumous medical degrees.

Set against the background of the suffrage movement, this book follows the struggle and determination of six Edinburgh women in the 1880's, who are striving to be allowed to train as doctors.

This is the first in a series of novels, which will deal with women's issues, such as equal rights to education and the parliamentary franchise, as the 19th century ends and the 20th century begins. I hope you enjoy reading about Letty and discovering what befalls her and her companions in their fight to become doctors.

I have learned so much, during the writing of this book, about the inequalities between the sexes and classes, in late Victorian society. I hope it will give the reader some food for thought.

Kay Race, October 2021

MAIN CHARACTERS

Mrs Louisa Frobisher (Nee Lady Louisa Moncrieff)

Dr Charles Frobisher - Louisa's husband

Evangeline Frobisher - daughter of Louisa and Charles

Harvey - Louisa's greyhound/ deerhound lurcher

Matilda - Evangeline's greyhound

Letitia (Letty) Frobisher - Charle's sister and Louisa's best friend

Dr Wilf Cunningham - Physician and tutor

Lord James and Lady Emily Moncrieff - Louisa's parents

Charlotte and Henry Frobisher - parents of Charles and Letty

Professor Smithson - Dean of the Faculty of Medicine, Edinburgh University

Professor Pilkington - Vehemently opposed to women doctors, Faculty of Medicine

Mrs Hammond - the Frobishers' housekeeper

Maggie - housemaid to the Frobishers

Rose Buchan - girl who was rescued from the Gideon Gentleman's Club

Detective Inspector Mike Wilkie - Edinburgh CID

Superintendent Beaton - Edinburgh Constabulary

1

4 HATTON PLACE
FRIDAY 25TH MARCH 1887

Louisa squeezed Charles's hand in a vice-like grip as another contraction came and she felt as though she was being ripped open.

She had been in labour for twelve hours and she was becoming weak from the pain and effort of bringing her baby into the world. Her usually lustrous auburn hair hung limp across the snow-white pillow and wisps of curls clung to her forehead, which was damp with beads of perspiration.

"Don't push yet Louisa, remember to pant - like Harvey!" said Charles.

This caused Louisa to laugh, slightly hysterically, but she did as he asked. Harvey was their lurcher and Louisa's devoted companion.

Men were usually banished from the labour room but Charles was a doctor, a well-qualified consultant, who had done his training in Obstetrics and Gynaecology as well as Paediatrics, his own sphere of expertise.

In general, doctors did not attend births unless there was a problem. They felt it was beneath them and it was left in the hands of midwives and nurses to look after women in labour.

Louisa and Charles had carefully planned the home delivery of their firstborn and their physician had agreed to his attendance on his wife.

"You're doing so well Louisa darling," said Lady Moncrieff, Louisa's mother, who was at the opposite side of the bed soothing her daughter's brow with cool damp flannels.

Charles had engaged Sister McNally, a midwife from the Royal Infirmary. Her high standard of professionalism, combined with compassion for her patients, made her the best person, in Charles's opinion, to help deliver their baby.

Sister McNally was at the foot of the bed monitoring Louisa's contractions and waiting for the baby to crown. Louisa cried out as another agonising contraction gripped her. Grabbing Charles's hand tighter, she panted breathlessly, "How long now Charles?"

"Can you see the baby's head yet Sister McNally?" Charles asked.

"Not yet Dr Frobisher, but I don't think we'll wait long for your son or daughter to make an appearance," she replied cheerily. Frances McNally was in her forties and had over twenty years experience of bringing babies into the world.

There was another anguished cry from Louisa as another, even more, excruciating contraction siezed her. She screamed through clenched teeth, "Please make that the last one, I can't bear any more pain."

"Please Louisa," said Charles, taking a small bottle of chloroform from his medical bag, "take just a few drops of this my love, it will help with the pain."

"No Charles, I won't have the foul stuff!" and she cried

out once more. Louisa had been kidnapped two years earlier and her captors had used an excessive amount of chloroform to render her unconscious. During their many discussions on labour and childbirth, Louisa had been adamant that she would not have it.

At that moment the midwife's no-nonsense voice announced, "I can see the head coming now, push all you want now m'dear Mrs Frobisher."

"It's really happening Charles, the baby is coming," gasped Louisa, with a mixture of laughter and tears as she pushed for all she was worth.

"You're doing really well Mrs Frobisher, keep pushing, that's the head now."

"Charles kissed Louisa's hand and then he noticed concern on the midwife's face.

"What's wrong Sister?" he asked as he left Louisa's side and went to where the midwife was holding the baby's head.

"The cord is around the baby's neck and I fear further pushing will only tighten it. I'll have to try to loosen it if we're to save your baby."

Charles nodded and quickly scrubbed his hands and wrists with carbolic soap in the hot water that had been brought up at regular intervals throughout the day.

As he did so, he said, "Louisa, I need you to stop pushing now. Please go back to panting for the next few moments."

"Is the baby alright Charles? What's wrong?" Her voice was raised in panic at this new and frightening development.

Her mother, doing her best to hide her own fear, murmured soothing words whilst looking anxiously at Charles.

Charles summed up the situation in an instant. The

baby was beginning to turn blue and there wasn't a second to waste.

He fired instructions to the midwife as he took instruments from his bag.

"Hold the baby's head Sister while I try to loosen the cord. He slipped his fingers around the little shoulder that was just appearing and felt the cord slacken. He quickly clamped and cut it.

"Start pushing again Louisa, you're nearly there," he said as Louisa continued to push her baby into the world.

Presently, his daughter slipped into his hands and he wrapped her in a soft towel, clearing the mucus from her little nose and mouth.

The baby made no sound and Louisa cried in alarm, "What's happening Charles? Why isn't the baby crying?" She turned to her mother as Charles was concentrating on the infant and did not answer her. "Mother, what's going on? Tell me, is my baby stillborn?"

Her mother, who'd had three stillbirths before Louisa's safe arrival, tried to hide the pain she was feeling that her only child may have lost this baby. But she let Louisa know nothing of this, instead she said, "Louisa, your baby is in the best possible hands with Charles and Sister McNally."

All the while, Charles was massaging the baby's tiny chest and was praying to God, with every fibre, to save his daughter. A memory came to him of something he had read in the Lancet a while back and he said, "Sister, fetch a basin of cold water and have someone bring more hot water up."

The midwife ran from the room to do his bidding and he continued to massage the little chest.

Sister McNally was back with the cold water in less than a minute.

"Put it on the dresser and bring the warm water there

too," said Charles as he gently laid the child into the basin of cold water and then into the warm water. Still there was no sound or movement from the child. He repeated the process while the women in the room looked on in astonished anguish. Suddenly, the baby took a shuddering breath and let out the most wonderful piercing wail. He quickly dried the crying child and wrapped her snugly in the little shawl that had been laid out in readiness more than twelve hours ago.

He laid the baby in Louisa's arms and said, "Louisa, we have a beautiful baby girl."

There were tears of joy and relief from everyone in the room, including the midwife, who had seen many wonderful things in all her years in midwifery, but nothing like this.

"This is nothing short of a miracle Dr Frobisher, well done!" she exclaimed.

Louisa looked at her daughter and asked, "Is she alright Charles?"

"She is well," he said, nodding and looking adoringly at mother and child. "I will examine her more closely in a little while, but now she needs her mother."

Her little rosebud mouth was searching for her first feed and while Louisa put her to the breast, the big blue eyes looked up trustingly at her mother as she sucked noisily.

Lady Moncrieff came over from where she had been sitting, out of the way of Charles and the midwife. She looked affectionately at her daughter and granddaughter and said, "I'll leave you now and get some tea and toast sent up to you. Well done darling girl," she added as she gently stroked the baby's cheek.

After the baby had been fed, Charles took his daughter to her crib to examine her. While he was doing that the midwife washed Louisa and helped her put on clean nightwear. She said, "That must feel a lot better Mrs Frobisher, all clean and comfy eh?"

"Indeed Sister," Louisa replied, "it feels wonderful, thank you."

When she was comfortable she said to Charles, "Is she alright Charles?"

"She is perfect Louisa," he said, looking at her little fingers and toes with the tiny white nails. He gently stroked her head and the soft hair that he thought would surely become the same radiant colour as her mother's. He was suddenly seized by an emotion that was so strong it took him by surprise. In that instant he realised two things: the first was that he was totally in love with this tiny scrap of humanity that his and Louisa's love for each other had produced; and the second thing was the almost overwhelming responsibility he felt would remain with him for the rest of his life.

He wrapped her up again and put her into Louisa's arms. Sister McNally had packed up her medical bag and she said, "I'll leave you now Dr Frobisher, Mrs Frobisher. Send for me if you need me." She smiled at Louisa and the baby and added, "but I don't think you will."

"Thank you Sister McNally, from the bottom of our hearts." The woman had remained cool and calm during the traumatic life and death crisis.

"Yes indeed, thank you Sister." Louisa added.

"What are we going to call her?" asked Charles, adding quickly, "I know we decided on Emily or Charlotte, after our mothers, if we had a girl, but if you're agreeable Louisa, I would like us to name our daughter Evangeline."

"Evangeline?" asked Louisa. She rolled the name around her tongue and repeated, "Evangeline. Yes Charles, I like the name, although I don't know anyone called Evangeline. Where does it come from?"

Charles stroked his sleeping baby's cheek and said softly, "It comes from the latin and means "good news"." He looked at Louisa and smiled, "and she is the best news we have ever had, especially after her struggle to be born."

Childbirth was very risky in Victorian times and maternal mortality was high. Women often died from infections following delivery. Although Charles had said nothing to Louisa about this, he was going to keep a close eye on his beloved wife in the coming days and weeks.

Evangeline, who was a honeymoon baby, like so many during this era, was a fortunate little girl to be born into the wealthier class. She would not suffer from hunger, as did many of the babies and children of the city's poorest, nor would any childhood illnesses go untreated through lack of money for doctor's fees or medicines.

As well as a life ahead of her among the privileged classes, she had been born to parents with progressive views, who believed that little girls and women should have the same opportunities as little boys and men. This included having equal access to a university education and votes for women, whereby they would have a say in who represented them in Parliament.

EVANGELINE'S PARENTS, Lady Louisa Moncrieff and Dr Charles Frobisher had married in June 1886. During the previous October (1885), in the course of her charitable work with the city's abused and neglected children, she had unwittingly stumbled on the illicit trade in young girls. This subsequently led to her being kidnapped and held captive in the basement of a townhouse which was being used for child prostitution.

Fortunately, due to Louisa having reported her concerns to them, the police were able to apprehend those guilty of using and providing this illicit trade. Louisa was rescued in the process of the police operation.

With all of that behind them, Louisa and Charles were looking forward to enjoying family life with their precious baby girl.

2

LETTY

Letitia Amelia Frobisher, Louisa's sister-in-law and called "Letty" by friends and family, was absolutely delighted by the arrival of Evangeline, making her an aunt for the first time.

"Aunt Letty," she thought to herself, "yes, I like the sound of that."

Letty was Charles's sister and had been Louisa's best friend since they were at school and, therefore, she was a natural choice as a Godmother to baby Evangeline.

Louisa was still confined to bed, but she had recovered well from her hours of labour two days before, and the new mother looked more radiant than ever.

Her satin-like auburn hair had been freshly washed and was arranged in a very becoming style by Margaret, her personal maid, and she wore a pale green crocheted bed shawl over her snow-white cotton nightdress. She looked the picture of health and happiness in the midst of the big mahogany four-poster bed, with its gold brocade curtains draped around it.

She sat propped up by a mound of pillows, cradling the

baby in her arms when Letty was shown into the room by Margaret and her face lit up when she saw her friend.

"Come in and meet your niece Letty," invited Louisa smiling.

Letty crossed the room and kissed Louisa's cheek. "You look wonderful Louisa," she said, "I was expecting you to be very tired and weak after your traumatic delivery. Charles told us all about it, you poor girl!" She looked at the baby in Louisa's arms and exclaimed, "Oh Louisa, she is utterly beautiful and adorable! Charles said that you have called her Evangeline." She gently stroked the soft cheek of the sleeping baby and added, "A beautiful name for your beautiful daughter."

"Would you care to hold her Letty?" Louisa asked.

Letty was both delighted and anxious at the unexpected offer. "May I? Oh but I'm afraid I might drop her."

"Nonsense," said Louisa, ringing the bell-pull by her bed. "Sit down on that chair and Nurse Mary will place Evangeline in your arms."

Letty sat down on the low gold-coloured nursing chair which matched the bed canopy, as the nurse entered the room.

"Mary," said Louisa, "this is Evangeline's aunt and Dr Frobisher's sister." Louisa was always inclusive in her dealings with her staff, as she had been during her time at her Children's Refuge and Homes. She believed it made for a more equal and harmonious working relationship.

Mary nodded and said, "Miss Frobisher."

Mary had been recruited by Charles and Louisa to help look after their precious baby from birth and for the first few years of their daughter's life. She was a woman in her mid-thirties with many years experience as a nursery nurse at the Royal Hospital for Sick Children and had come with excellent testimonials.

Letty smiled and said, "Hello Mary, it's good to meet you."

"Mary, would you please put baby Evangeline into her aunt's arms, she is going to hold her for a little while."

Mary gently and expertly took her from Louisa and put her into a nervous Letty's arms, making sure that her little head was supported.

Aunt Letty began to relax once Evangeline was placed in her arms and she breathed in the lovely baby smell.

"Hello Evangeline," she said softly, "I'm your Aunt Letty and I'm going to teach you to become a great suffragist and social reformer."

Louisa laughed, saying, "She's a bit young for the vote Letty."

"It's never to soon to start your education regarding votes and access to medical training for women, is it my darling?"

"Besides," continued Louisa, "we should have the vote by the time she will be old enough to campaign for it."

"Amen to that." said Letty, looking up from the baby to Louisa. "but if we haven't been granted the right to vote by the time she is of age, that will mean there will have been generations of Frobishers and Moncrieffs campaigning for it." She looked at Evangeline and added, "Although it's very discouraging to think that we might still not have the franchise when this little girl is old enough to vote for a member of parliament. Do you realise Louisa that it will be 1908 when Evangeline is twenty-one. Surely we will have the vote by then!"

"Let's not get carried away into the twentieth century Letty, we don't want to wish her time away. I want to enjoy Evangeline's babyhood and childhood each and every day."

She looked at the baby, asleep in her sister-in-law's arms, and asked, "How are the studies coming along Letty?"

Letty had asked Charles if he knew of anyone who would be willing to tutor her and some friends in the courses required to apply for medical training. They were most fortunate in engaging the services of a doctor friend of Charles and they had hired a room in the Royal High School three nights a week over the past six months, studying anatomy, physiology, chemistry and mathematics. They had all studied Latin at school and on the Higher Certificate at Edinburgh University some years before.

" Very well indeed," Letty smiled enthusiastically, "We have successfully completed all our assignments and Dr Cunningham said we should pass the matriculation examination, that is, if our applications are successful and we are permitted to sit it."

"I wish you the very best of luck Letty, we both know many women who would prefer to see a woman doctor, but at this point in time, I'm afraid we have no choice. She looked at Evangeline, still sleeping peacefully in Letty's arms and added, "I hope this little girl will not encounter such outrageous opposition and prejudice if she chooses to follow in her father's footsteps."

Just then the baby began to stir and become restive. "Perhaps you should ring for her nurse, I think she may need to have her napkin changed."

Once Mary had taken Evangeline to the nursery to change her, Letty asked, "Has Charles gone back to work?"

"He has but he comes in several times a day to make sure both the baby and I are still well and not in any distress."

"That sounds just like my brother," Letty quipped.

"I keep telling him that we are well and not to fuss like an old mother hen and that a lunchtime visit would suffice.

It's just as well we live so close to the hospital" After a few moments thought, she added, uncertain, "You don't think there's something that could go wrong with the baby and he's not telling me so as not to worry me, do you Letitia?" The fact that she'd called her friend by her full name, revealed some apprehension on Louisa's part.

"Not at all Louisa," Letty replied quickly, "it's just Charles's way," and to reinforce her assurances added, "you've been with Charles long enough to know how meticulous and conscientious he is about his patients and family, so please don't let your imagination run away with you."

Charles was a Consultant Paediatrician at the Sick Children's Hospital and made all the arrangements for Louisa's lying-in after giving birth.

"Mother is coming to coming to see you this afternoon, I hope having us both visit you in the one day won't be too much for you Louisa?"

"It won't, don't worry. I'm going to have lots of rest before then."

"That's alright then," said Letty, satisfied."Well I must love you and leave you my dear as I have a meeting with the others from the study group. We are going to make contingency plans should our application to sit the matriculation examination be rejected."

"I admire your courage Letty. There are so many issues regarding women's rights, apart from getting the vote, it seems that women are constantly campaigning for one thing or another."

"We are getting wonderful support from our members in the Edinburgh Suffrage branch - and elsewhere, as a matter of fact. If we are refused admission to the medical degree course, there will be a protest rally outside the School of

Medicine whilst I and my fellow students will make a deputation to the Dean of the Faculty.

"You will make a wonderful doctor Letty," said Louisa but before you go, I want to tell you that Charles and I would like you to be Evangeline's Godmother. Would you?" We're still considering who to ask to be her Godfather, but we both want you to be her Godmother."

Letty was surprised and absolutely delighted to be chosen as a godparent to their first child. "I'd love to, thank you for considering me to be suitable for such a responsibility." She hugged Louisa, tears of joy in her eyes.

"We both believe that, with you as her Godmother, she will be well-guided throughout her life." Louisa said as she hugged her back.

"Now go to your meeting Letty dear and thank you for your visit." She kissed Letty's cheek and her sister-in-law left for her meeting, feeling as though she was walking on air.

LETTY WAS the middle child in the Frobisher family and the only girl. She was a petite woman, just over five feet tall, with the blonde hair and blue eyes which she and Charles had inherited from their mother. She was an attractive woman with a keen intelligence and a positive outlook on life. However she also had a tenacity which, at times, put her at loggerheads with her parents, particularly her father.

Over the years she'd often railed against her parents for not letting her do what Charles, the oldest child, and even worse still, George who was six years her junior, were allowed to do. Despite her parents regarding themselves as having progressive views, Letty felt that these were more in the nature of lip service when it came to her, and she often relied on Charles to be in her corner when there was a dispute or parental disapproval of something she wanted to participate in. She didn't have a "chip on her shoulder", but was acutely alert to any differences as to how she was treated in the family, especially if the only reason she was being prevented from doing something was purely because she was a female. This awareness of gender acceptance or exclusion strengthened her determination to campaign for equal rights, both within and outside the home.

More than a decade earlier, women were not permitted to study at Edinburgh University and, as soon as the University opened its doors to women, allowing them to enrol in an Arts Certificate, Letty wanted to go on the course. Her parents were rather dubious about whether to let their daughter go, but Charles had persuaded them to agree, thus Letty and Louisa were among the first students to enrol.

Equal access to degree courses was one of the many women's rights issues that their mothers' generation had, for many years, been campaigning for and, although the university still denied degrees to women, this was considered a step towards that goal. However, it would be well into the 1890's before women would be accepted onto degree courses.

Letty and Louisa joined various societies including the The Edinburgh Women's Suffrage Association, the Fabian Society and the Edinburgh Women's Debating Society. The latter provided an excellent opportunity to speak publicly without incurring the scorn of men and stood them in good stead as public speakers for any campaigns they might become involved in. Their mothers had been members of the Edinburgh Suffrage Association since its inception in 1867.

The Fabian Society appealed to both young women, who had grown up in families with progressive views on social justice and women's suffrage. There were often heated discussions in the meetings on topics such as universal franchise and the best way to engage working class women and men in their campaigns. Louisa often found herself defending her work with the abused and neglected children, which was dismissed as "just a drop in the vast ocean of suffering humanity".

She would reply with a resolute, "It may well be a tiny deed in the larger scale of things, but for those individual children I help, it could be life-changing or even life-saving."

Although Letty and Louisa's interests diverged later, they remained best friends and supported each other's campaigns and fundraising events.

As the eighth decade of the nineteenth century wore on, Letty became more involved in the campaign to allow women equal access to medical training as men. She had yearned for many years to become a doctor, like her brother Charles and even her much younger brother, George, who had gained his degree in medicine, whilst she and hundreds of women, were denied the opportunity. Letty felt this injustice acutely.

Thus, she and five friends who shared her burning ambition to become a doctor, had been engaged in an intensive course of study in order to equip them to sit and pass the matriculation examination as the means onto the medical degree course.

From the many debates, both in the context of the Women's Debating Society and within the suffrage movement, it was widely recognised that, even if individual women themselves had no interest in becoming doctors, they all wanted access to female doctors.

The same questions were being asked by both the

women's suffrage movement and the campaign for the higher education of women. Why were the men who ran these institutions so against women having equal access to a degree course; or to vote for a parliamentary representative?

Whatever the answer to these questions might be, it was clear that women, including Letty and Louisa, would continue to campaign and petition for the right to vote and the right to become doctors.

3

THE MATRICULATION EXAMINATION AND VILIFICATION

APRIL 1887

It was the last evening class for the study group in room 5 of the Royal High School on the Calton Hill.

Dr Cunningham, their tutor, was very impressed by the application and dedication of these women who wanted to gain a place at the Medical School of Edinburgh University.

"Ladies, you have all excelled in your studies and the deliberately difficult assignments I have given you over the past six months. I have every confidence that you will all do well in the matriculation examination on Wednesday."

His six students chorused, "Thank you Dr Cunningham." They believed they would do well and were encouraged by his words.

"Goodnight and let me know how you find the test papers."

Letty, who had hired the tutor on behalf of the group, said "Dr Cunningham, we all want to thank you for your excellent teaching methods, your patience and your belief in our ability. We shall endeavour to make you proud of us."

Then all six women gave him a round of applause before

saying goodnight and leaving the classroom for the last time.

Charles had been right when he said that he knew the best person for the job when Letty had approached him about finding a tutor in the autumn of the previous year.

Wilfred Cunningham (Wilf to his intimates) had been at Edinburgh Academy with Charles and had been in his peer group at medical school. He had gone into general practice and was, in Charles words, "a brilliant diagnostician." Like Charles, he was also a member of the Men's League for Votes for Women, as well as believing in their right to train as doctors.

Even Letty's parents approved, which surprised her since they'd had to be persuaded by Charles to allow her to enrol in the university's new Higher Certificate of Education course in the 1870's. Although progressive in their views, her parents were rather more cautious than her best friend, Louisa's, had been throughout their friendship. Of course, she was much older now and they knew how keen she was to follow her brothers into medicine.

Letty and her five fellow students: Emmeline Franks, Marion McNair, Juliette Whitton, Victoria Browne and Jessica Wilmott met at the statue of Greyfriar's Bobby, on the corner of George IV Bridge and Candlemaker Row, on the morning of Wednesday 20th April.

They had decided to meet as a group, rather than arrive in the examination hall individually. "Strength in numbers." Letty had said, "We need all the psychological advantage we can muster."

They were indeed glad they went into the hall together since there was much curiosity and even laughter, when the invigilator met them and directed them to their seats.

"Quiet gentlemen please!" he said sternly. He then

placed an examination paper face-down on each desk. The time was a minute to nine when he announced, "You may turn your examination papers over now, you have three hours to complete your test paper. If you finish early, do not leave the room since this will distract the other students. When you are finished, please remain in your seats until you are dismissed. You may begin."

Letty and her companions wrote industriously for the three hours. They were pleased that the questions were on the topics that they had studied with Doctor Cunningham: anatomy; physiology; chemistry; mathematics and Latin. Even if the surroundings were totally alien to them, the subjects were certainly familiar and they felt as at ease as it was possible to be, whilst taking the most important examination of their lives so far.

THE RESULTS of the matriculation examination were to be posted on the Medical School notice board on the 27th April. It was with some trepidation that Letty and her friends approached the Medical School in Teviot Row, accompanied by Doctor Cunningham.

The notice board was in the foyer of the building and, as they walked through the door, a number of young men were clustered around the results. One of the men, nearest the board, was pointing at the list, exclaiming, "That can't be right, there must be some mistake!"

Another pushed in and said, "Too fucking true Simpson, that cannot be right."

At the expletive, Wilf cleared his throat noisily and said, "Gentlemen, that is no language to use in front of ladies."

They turned around quickly to see that everything they

said had been witnessed by the six women and the man they knew to be an eminent Edinburgh physician.

They hurried past the group of women, almost shoving them, in their rush to get through the door. However, they were not fast enough to hide the emotions expressed on their faces. Some were embarrassed, but there were two or three who looked with brazen hostility at Letty and her friends.

Standing in front of the board, they read the source of their disbelief and dismay, for all six had surpassed the men in their examination results. Their marks ranged from ninety-eight percent to ninety-three percent, whereas the top mark amongst the men was a mere ninety percent.

They hugged and congratulated each other, almost dancing with joy. They found themselves babbling to each other: "Gosh, I never thought I would do so well" and "I thought I would pass, but I never thought by that much" and from Letty, "Me too, I thought I would pass but I never dreamt I would come top of the class!"

She turned to Wilf and hugged him, saying, "Thank you, thank you so much Doctor Cunningham." At this, the others chorused, "Yes, thank you Doctor Cunningham."

Wilf's face was illuminated by his wide smile of delight. He said, "Congratulations to the class of '87! I knew you would do well and you have indeed excelled." He beamed at each and every one of them. "You've certainly given those young pups a run for their money," he indicated the door that the young men had hastily exited through a few minutes before.

"You do realise what this means, don't you?" he asked.

Emmeline Franks, who had come third with ninety-six percent said, "Yes of course, Dr Cunningham. We've passed and will be admitted to the medical degree course."

"Yes, that too Miss Franks," replied their tutor, "but the four entrants with the highest marks are awarded the Hope Scholarship, and so, your fees will be paid along with a subsistence allowance for lodgings and textbooks."

"Oh my," said Letty, "in the excitement of passing we had all forgotten that."

"In fact," added Marion McNair, who had scored ninety-seven percent, "I had dismissed the idea from my mind, as far back as our first tutorials, since although I hoped I would pass, I had no notion that I would get a mark over sixty percent, or maybe seventy at most," she laughed and added, "a scholarship will make such a difference, since it's been a bit difficult since Father's sudden death two years ago." Her face clouded as she said this and Wilf said, in a very gentle, sympathetic tone, "Miss McNair, I know your dear father would be very proud of you right now."

They began to move back outside into the quadrangle as more hopefuls came in to look at their results.

Wilf said, "Let's go to the coffee house on George IV Bridge before you all go home with your wonderful news. It will be my treat."

"Wonderful idea Sir," said Jessica Wilmott, "Can you run to scones as well?" she added with an impish grin.

"You can have anything you like ladies, you won't come across an occasion like this too often, in fact, I've never heard of it before."

In the coffee house, Wilf watched as they all chatted away happily like a group of schoolgirls, rather than women in their twenties. A niggling feeling, that began as they had encountered the disgruntled young men at the notice board, surfaced again. He hated himself for what he was about to say, but he knew he would be nothing short of disingenuous if he did not mention what was troubling him.

He cleared his throat It had been his way of getting attention in the class, and was a rather endearing quality in the mild-mannered man. They all stopped talking at once and looked at him expectantly.

He said, "I am the last one to pour cold water onto your happiness, but I think you should take something into consideration in relation to studying medicine in, virtually, an all male environment."

Letty, always quick on the uptake and who hadn't wanted to spoil the joyous mood of her friends, said, "It's to do with those young men at the notice board, isn't it Dr Cunningham?"

He nodded, "Yes, you may have seen or felt their hostility at the results of the examination. I don't think they appreciated being beaten by women ..."

Letty interrupted him and said in a grim tone, "Well it gives a lie to the age-old argument that women are intellectually inferior to men."

Dr Cunningham nodded and continued, "Yes, but I think it is only right that you are prepared for this when your course begins in October.

IN THE WEEK THAT FOLLOWED, a veritable storm developed in the newspapers. Hostility to women being allowed to do a medical degree at Edinburgh University grew and was believed to be fuelled, to a large extent, by Professor Pilkington, from the Medical School, who was vehemently opposed to women doctors. He refuted the claim that many women wanted to be treated by female doctors and, in a letter to the editor of the *Scotsman* newspaper on the 30th of April, he wrote:

. . .

"Sir,

I must put to rest this absurd notion of women saying that they wish to be treated by female doctors. My own enquiries lead me to believe that the opposite is true.

Furthermore, women's natures are not suited to the rigours of a medical career. They are too physically, mentally and emotionally frail to undergo the training and hard work of being a physician or surgeon, God forbid!

I might even suggest that the type of female wishing to pursue a career in medicine must be of a base nature or "Magdalenes". I will not countenance such a class of person to be permitted to enter our hallowed halls.

Finally, there is no, nor will there ever be, a facility for females to be accommodated in the practical training carried out on the wards of the Royal Infirmary.

In conclusion, I say to you women, become midwives, not doctors!

Sincerely, et cetera, et cetera,

Edward P Pilkington

Professor of Medicine, University of Edinburgh.

THE WOMEN, their families and supporters were appalled and incensed by the spiralling vitriol towards them and Charles had heard, on good authority from his contacts in the Medical Faculty, that Professor Pilkington was inciting the young men in their opposition and naked hostility to the women who had done so much better than them in the examination.

Letters were published daily in the *Scotsman* and the *Edinburgh Evening News*, from people against admitting the women, and also from those who were for female doctors.

Hundreds of women had written to the newspapers stating their preference for women physicians.

One such letter for the women was sent anonymously, it read:

"Sir,

I wish to take issue with Professor Pilkington in regard to his letter of 30th April. His views are a weak attempt to veil a deep and pathological dislike of women, in fact, one might reasonably call him a misogynist. He obviously has some innate fear of women being allowed into positions of power or authority, possibly, as a child, he suffered at the hands of a sadistic nanny.

His statements that women are, to use his own words, "physically, emotionally and mentally frail" are not supported with evidence, particularly scientific evidence, which is rather poor coming from a man of science and a medical professor at that. It has been well demonstrated by the six women who sat the matriculation examination and who all attained marks higher than any of the men who sat the same test, that his argument for mental or intellectual frailty is based on a false premise.

Finally, his reference to women wishing to be doctors as having "base natures" is somewhat confusing, not to mention illogical. Do the men who are allowed to enter his "hallowed halls" to train as doctors, have base natures? I rather think he would deny this, so then, why would the women? Likewise, his allusion to them being "Magdalenes", demonstrates an appalling lack of compassion for those poor souls who are afflicted with poor mental health and who have to seek shelter at asylums founded to help such unfortunates.

In conclusion, Professor Pilkington is spouting his vitriol from a predisposition of prejudice against women as a sex and nothing else.

Sincerely,

A sympathiser of the Edinburgh Six"

THE NEWSPAPERS, who had been alerted anonymously, of the women's success in the entry examination and whose first letters had been extremely hostile to them, came down firmly on the side of having female doctors, as the following editorial shows.

"DEAR READERS

We have had an overwhelming amount of correspondence regarding those for, and against, women doctors. Those in favour of having women being accepted for medical training far outnumbers those who are against it.

Indeed the letters received are interesting in themselves. Those received from, both men and women, were far more articulate and had well-reasoned arguments supporting their case. In contrast to this, the 'antis', if I may call them that, have a tendency to use unproven statements of the sort mentioned before, such as the "fact" - untested and unproven - that women are physically, mentally and emotionally frail. Many, many women, especially those in the poorer classes, do work involving hard physical labour as well as running their homes for their children and husbands. In addition, women of all classes who bear children undergo much hard work and pain that I fear men would not wish to undergo, supposing it was possible.

The "Edinburgh Six" prove that women are not intellectually inferior, having outdone all the males sitting the same matriculation examination. It would seem that those against allowing women to study medicine are expressing feelings of "sour grapes and prejudice" and cannot find any rational argument that would stand up.

We salute and admire these six women whose courage and intelligence has been rewarded, we wish them every success in their studies and future careers."

CHARLES A. COOPER EDITOR, Scotsman Newspaper

4

HOPE, THEN HOPE DASHED
A MEETING WITH THE DEAN

A week later, Letty and her five companions received identical letters. The pertinent part read:

"The Faculty of Medicine and the University Court has agreed, on closer consideration, and in the light of strong opposition, that our recently-announced policy of admitting women for medical training has been reviewed and rescinded. This means that the Hope Scholarship, and the automatic acceptance on passing the matriculation examination, has also been revoked."

With the finality of the rejections, Letty and the others met to revisit their contingency plan of appealing to the Dean of the Faculty.

Letty wrote, in her opinion, the most sickeningly ingratiating letter to the Dean, asking if he would be willing to meet the women to explain the situation face to face. In the letter she said,

"This decision will have a profound effect on our lives. We took the examination on the understanding that, if we passed, we would be admitted to the medical training course. There is obviously no issue over our ability, given our test marks, so it would be enormously appreciated if you would meet with us and explain how, what should have been automatic admission, has been revoked, with no opportunity of appeal."

ON THE 4TH OF MAY, to their surprise, he wrote agreeing to meet the deputation on Friday the 13th of May at ten o'clock, in his office at the School of Medicine. This gave them just over a week to organise support from their suffrage sisters, as well as from the Men's League for Votes for Women.

The debate on the "Women's Question" as it had been named, continued unabated in the press. They decided not to inform the papers about their meeting with the Dean, so as to avoid any further hostility.

There would be a peaceful demonstration, outside the Medical School, by the Edinburgh Branch of the Women's Suffrage Association, with banners calling for "Equal Rights" and "Votes for Women".

The morning of the thirteenth dawned fair and bright, which Letty and the others took to be a good omen. Over fifty suffragists and fifteen men gathered at the corner of Chambers Street and George IV Bridge to escort the six women on the short walk to the Medical School in Teviot Place.

Unknown to the deputation and demonstrators, Professor Pilkington had fuelled the fire of intolerance and hostility towards the women and had leaked to students the date and time time that the women would be meeting with the Dean.

As the group turned from Bristo Place into Teviot Place, they met an angry mob of medical students and would-be medical students, about fifty in number, who had sat the matriculation examination.

All at once there were jeers and swearing at the women from the young men carrying boards and chanting, "Go back to your homes where you belong", "whores" and "Magdalenes".

The men from the Men's League, who traditionally followed a procession, quickly placed themselves between the suffragists and the angry young men. Dr Cunningham, on first spotting the trouble ahead, sent someone to the nearest police station for help.

The women in the procession, like Letty and her friends, kept their heads held high, looked straight ahead and continued to walk calmly to the entrance of the Medical School. They were used to foul-mouthed men, jeering and swearing, from their many suffragist processions and marches in Edinburgh and other cities.

The noise from the counter-demonstrators brought the university servitors out from the booth at the entrance to the medical school quadrangle and they remonstrated with the angry mob.

Although perceived as lowly people, servitors, especially amongst medical students, were nevertheless respected as they were key holders to laboratories and libraries and did the well-off young students favours after doors were closed.

Ted, the senior of the two men, called to the men to be quiet. "Gentlemen, silence please! These young ladies have an appointment with the Dean, who I am sure would disapprove of such ungentlemanly behaviour." They were silenced and some were shame-faced at the servitor's words. "Now let these ladies pass. Fred," he said to his colleague, "please take these ladies to Professor Smithson's office."

Dr Cunningham had, at his students' invitation, agreed

to accompany his proteges and hopefully to help plead their case more forcefully than they might do, given he had been through medical training and was a well-respected practitioner in Edinburgh.

While Fred was taking the small deputation to the Dean's office, Ted persuaded the counter-demonstrators to move away and the fifty-five suffragists stood in silent vigil waiting for their friends to return.

"Thank you for agreeing to this meeting Professor Smithson, we do appreciate you making time to speak to us," said Letty who, by tacit agreement, was their spokesperson. She then introduced herself and the others to him.

"It is both a pleasure and a sorrow to me ladies, since I do not have news that will encourage you, I"m afraid," said the Dean, who looked genuinely sorry.

They were seated in his large office on the top floor of the building, which overlooked Middle Meadow Walk and the Royal Infirmary, which stood on the opposite side of the Walk. It was a bright, airy room with three wood-panelled walls. The remaining wall had floor to ceiling bookshelves filled with medical and classical tomes.

Letty and her friends were in awe of the atmosphere of intellectual excellence and the Dean made an effort to make them feel at ease.

"May I congratulate you all in achieving such high marks in the matriculation examination," he began, "it has been a long time since an applicant got such high marks in an entrance exam and, may I say, that it proves that women are not intellectually inferior to men - not that I ever subscribed to such a stupid notion."

Dr Cunningham said, "And yet, from your opening remarks, I assume despite their marks, these women will not be offered places on the medical training course."

"I"m afraid so, Dr Cunningham," said Professor Smithson sadly.

"Would it not have been better to have confirmed that decision in writing and saved them from the jeering and swearing that they have just encountered whilst trying to enter the building to keep their appointment with you?"

"Oh dear!" said the Dean, "this is very distressing, do you know who is responsible?"

"I am guessing that some are your students, Professor Smithson, and one or two sat the matriculation examination alongside my students," said Dr Cunningham. "The servitors who came out to see what the ruckus was, seemed to know the young men."

"I cannot apologise enough ladies and I shall see the culprits are reprimanded."

They all murmured a polite "thank you".

He went on, "I am extremely sorry that you have come here and suffered such unforgivable behaviour," he said, looking very sorry indeed, "If I'd had any idea that there was any possibility of such an occurrence, I would not have invited you here. As far as I am aware, no one other than my Faculty colleagues knew about this meeting."

"Yet, somehow those reprehensible young men found out, not just the day, but the time." said Dr Cunningham.

"That would seem to be the case and enquiries will also be made in that quarter too," he said, looking very thoughtful and solemn. "but please, permit me to say what it was that I invited you here to tell you. I wanted you to know that the University Court's decision to reject your application and forfeit your scholarships is final and I realise that you could have been informed by post. However, I wanted to meet the courageous women who entered an examination hall full of men, in order to pursue their ambition of becoming doctors. I personally, am in favour of training women to be doctors, but although I voted to allow you on the course, sadly I was outnumbered."

Letty said, "Thank you for those words Professor Smithson, it makes me feel better that, at least one person in the Faculty was on our side."

There followed, "thank you indeed Professor" and "yes, thank you" from Letty's friends.

Dr Cunningham stood up, signalling the end of the meeting. He shook hands with the Dean and thanked him again.

Letty said, "I think I speak for us all when I say that, despite the extremely bad behaviour of those men, it has been a pleasure meeting you and hearing your words of support for us."

"All I can say ladies is, that I hope the policy of not training women to be doctors is reversed in the very near future."

They all said goodbye and made their way downstairs and out of the building. When they came through the quadrangle archway and out onto Teviot Place, all was peaceful and the suffragists gave a big cheer. However, it died on their lips when they saw the women shake their heads in reply to their unspoken question.

Letty, as spokesperson again, addressed the men and women who had come out in support of them. She said, "Friends and sisters, thank you from the bottom of our hearts for your strength in numbers and for your empathy. We truly appreciate your support and solidarity. You displayed great dignity in the face of the vile hostility and, although the university will not change their position on training women to become doctors, we live to fight another day. Thank you."

A great cheer went up and, just then, Letty noticed two men writing away furiously in little notebooks. She asked Dr Cunningham, "Who are those men over there? Do you know them?"

He replied, "No, I don't but I would say that they are newspaper reporters"

"Well, it's a pity they weren't here thirty minutes ago, they'd have got a story then!" said Letty.

As the procession of suffragists and male supporters moved along Teviot Place towards the top of Middle Meadow Walk, the mob of angry students suddenly re-appeared. They had been lying in wait amongst the trees that lined the walkway.

They proceeded to lob rubbish and mud, as well as shouting insults and obscenities at the women.

The policemen that Wilf had sent someone for, had just arrived. They tried to intervene and reason with the students, but to no avail.

The women towards the back of the procession turned around and hurried in the opposite direction, leaving room for those at the front to retreat. Everyone was trying to get out the range of the missiles and passers-by ran for cover as the two constables tried, unsuccessfully, to bring the situation under control.

All the while, the men who had reached the front of the procession, were trying to usher the suffrage demonstrators back towards the safety of the Medical School, where those who had been at the rear were now gathering. By this time, police whistles could be heard as the outnumbered constables called for help from others in the vicinity.

Before any help arrived however, Letty was struck on the side of the head with a large stone. She was momentarily stunned and almost tumbled to the ground, under the feet of those hurrying back to safety. Luckily, Marion was beside her and stopped her from falling. She pulled her through the arch to the servitors' booth and into the safety of the building. Blood was running freely from the wound on Letty's head and Marion called out to Dr Cunningham that Letty was injured.

He quickly made his way across to her. Letty had removed her hat and Marion had a handkerchief pressed on the wound in an attempt to stem the bleeding.

Dr Cunningham asked, "How do you feel Miss Frobisher?" as he took her pulse. He then carefully lifted the handkerchief from her head in order to assess the damage. He replaced the make-do dressing with his own larger one and instructed Letty to hold it in place. "It doesn't look too bad, but I fear it will need some sutures. Do you feel up to walking? Fortunately the Royal Infirmary is only a few hundred yards away."

"Yes, I think I can manage that Dr Cunningham, but is it safe to go back out there again?"

Wilf called the servitor over and said, "Go out and see if it is safe to take this lady to the Royal Infirmary."

"Yes Sir," said Ted and hurried off.

Outside, Ted could see that reinforcements had arrived and several young men were handcuffed and being put into two police wagons, locally known as "Black Mariahs". The others had fled down towards the Meadows when they saw that more constables were arriving.

Ted returned to the servitor's lodge and said, "It is safe now Sir, several men have been arrested and the rest o' the cowardly thugs were runnin' doon the Walk like the Earl o' Hell hissel wis after them."

Letty smiled at the image his words conjured up, despite the throbbing in her head.

"Let's go Miss Frobisher, the sooner we get that wound cleaned and stitched, the better," urged Wilf.

"Do you want us to come with you Letty?" asked a worried looking Marion.

"It's probably best not to have too many people there," said Dr Cunningham, "we don't want to get in the way of the doctors and nurses."

"Why don't you all call round for tea tomorrow afternoon everyone?" said Letty, "and we can have a good old post mortem and decide where we go from here."

"Jolly good idea!" exclaimed Victoria, "but only if you think you'll be up to it."

"I ought to be by then," replied Letty as Wilf led her out.

Fortunately, they did not have long to wait at the hospital and Letty's wound was cleaned and sutured by a junior doctor, closely watched over by Wilf, who had seen enough of young medical men for one day.

5

THE AFTERMATH

Letty was released from hospital about forty minutes later, once the medics were sure that she wasn't suffering concussion. Wilf hailed a cab and took Letty home to Lauder Road in the affluent Grange area of Edinburgh.

Letty let herself into the house and invited Wilf to come in and meet her mother, who she knew was working from home on the next suffrage petition to parliament.

Her mother didn't look up right away when Letty entered the south-facing morning room, where her mother preferred to work, since it was brighter than her study.

She asked, "Well darling, how did it go? I hope they are doing the right thing and letting you girls back on the course." She looked up then, and when she saw the bandage on Letty's head and the blood on her coat, she ran to her daughter, horrified.

"Lord in heaven Letitia, what has happened to you?" Her mother always called her Letitia when she was stressed or anxious.

Letty touched her temple gingerly and said, "It's not as

bad as it looks Mother, don't worry so. I'm alright." She turned to Dr Cunningham and asked, "I am alright, aren't I?"

Her mother now noticed the man beside her daughter for the first time and Wilf felt the eyes of both women looking at him expectantly, waiting for an answer. He realised that Letty was inviting him to give her mother an account of what had happened.

"Mother, this is Dr Cunningham, our tutor, who was with us today to help plead our case to the Dean."

"I'm pleased to meet you Dr Cunningham," said Mrs Frobisher, shaking the proffered hand.

"I am glad to meet you too Mrs Frobisher," replied Wilf, who then gave her a summary of what had occurred outside the Medical School and Letty's subsequent injury.

"Despicable!" she exclaimed, incandescent with rage, "absolutely shocking behaviour! And those young men are supposed to come from better-off, educated families. Thugs! That is what they are, I'd like to take a whip to them."

"I feel exactly the same way, Mrs Frobisher," said Wilf, "but I believe between the police and the Dean of the Faculty, those responsible will be severely dealt with and I wouldn't be surprised if they are made an example of and are expelled from the university and their medical studies."

"One hopes so," said Mrs Frobisher, "but how did the meeting with the Dean go?" she asked Letty.

"He was very kind and he was in favour of us being allowed on the course, but he was out-voted. He was very impressed with our examination results too."

"It's absolutely scandalous, not giving you your rightful places and scholarships," she said with passion and added, "I suppose they'll go to those beastly boys."

Letty said that she was going to lie down for a few hours

as she was feeling very weak and a bit shaky from all the trauma.

"You go on up, Letty dear," said her mother, ""I'll look after Dr Cunningham."

When Letty had gone, having thanked Wilf for being with them, she asked, "Would you like some tea or coffee Dr Cunningham?"

"That's very kind of you Mrs Frobisher, but I have to get back to work. I left a locum doctor to look after the practice while I accompanied my students to the meeting with the Dean."

"Thank you for looking after Letitia, we're very grateful to you. I'll show you to the door."

Wilf said, "It was the least I could do. I'm only sorry that they were treated in such a brutal manner. It was totally unexpected, the more so when you think about the kind of homes they come from."

"Yes, it makes me wonder what the world is coming to."

"I agree with you. Letty should feel much better after a rest and some food. However, if she feels unwell I would advise you to contact your physician right away."

"Thank you again, Dr Cunningham, goodbye."

Charlotte Frobisher returned to the morning room and stared, unseeing, out of the window. She was wondering whether to try to persuade Letty to give up her ambition of becoming a doctor, if today's thuggery was any indication of the obstacles that lay ahead. "Charles and George sailed through their medical degrees, but then they are men. Perhaps this will be an end to it and I won't have to persuade her, she may already have made that decision herself," she thought, totally underestimating her daughter's ambition and determination.

Later that day

Henry Frobisher came home from work that evening with a copy of the *Edinburgh Evening News*. He had been about to walk past the newspaper boy at the crossroads of the High Street and George IV Bridge, since he rarely took the *News*, when the headline caught his eye. It read:

"Friday the 13th Indeed! **Women attacked by Angry Mob of Medical Students**"

He stood in the middle of the pavement and read the article with increasing dismay and horror.

"This morning, a deputation of six women were harassed by an angry mob of medical students, as they made their way to a meeting with the Dean of the Medical Faculty.

The women, who had achieved very high marks, higher than any of the men, in their entrance examination last month, had been refused admission to the medical degree course.

The issue of women doctors has been well-aired in this newspaper, as well as the *Scotsman,* with advocates from both sides making their views known.

The ladies were on their way to speak with the Dean to plead their case, and to ask if the University would reconsider its decision. But before they had even reached the Medical School, they were harangued by men using the most foul and lewd language. Despite such shocking behaviour, the ladies walked on with dignity, heads held high.

Two university servitors dispersed the crowd of around fifty students, admonishing then for their behaviour. The women were accompanied by over fifty members of the Edinburgh Women's Suffrage Association in a show of support and solidarity. They stood in dignified silence while the deputation attended their appointment with Professor Smithson, The Dean of the Faculty.

When they came out again, it was clear that their plea had been unsuccessful and Miss Letitia Frobisher, spokeswoman for the small deputation, thanked them for their support.

The procession had begun to walk away from the medical school when they were once again set upon by the angry students, only this time their anger was physical. They began pelting the women with mud and other foul missiles. Miss Frobisher was struck on the head with a stone and she sustained an injury requiring medical attention at the nearby Royal Infirmary.

Most of the women managed to reach the safety of the medical School quadrangle without serious harm. We interviewed two ladies from the deputation, Miss Jessica Wilmott and Miss Juliette Whitton, at the scene.

Miss Wilmott said, "The only word to describe those despicable young men is "thugs". They were not satisfied that we had been refused entry onto the medical degree course and I can only assume that such behaviour was caused by the fact that we *mere women* had achieved higher marks in the matriculation examination."

Miss Whitton added, "If "First do no harm" is the main article of the Hippocratic oath, then those men should have no place training to be doctors."

Although the two police constables were in attendance, there was only so much they could do being outnumbered by 50 to 2. It was when reinforcements arrived in two Black Mariahs, that arrests were made, however a number of the culprits made their escape in the direction of the Meadows. Those arrested are due to appear in court tomorrow and are being held in custody until then.

Gerald Knight, correspondent."

Henry Frobisher jumped out of the cab he had hailed at the Lawnmarket, quickly paid the driver and hurried into the house.

"Charlotte," he called, as he entered the house, "where is Letitia? Is she alright?"

"Come into the drawing room Henry and I'll tell you all about it."

She handed him a glass of brandy and poured one for herself. He sat down heavily on the sofa while she stood by the fireplace and told him, more or less, what he had read in the newspaper.

"And she's alright?" he asked again.

"Yes Henry, she's fine now. She has three stitches in the wound which will be removed in seven days time." She took a sip of her brandy and sat down in one of the armchairs by the fireside. The fire was unlit but the room was suffused with evening sunlight through the west-facing window. It was a restful room and was decorated in varying hues of blue. Since she'd been a small child, Letty had called it "The Blue Room".

Charlotte continued, "She slept most of the afternoon, poor dear. She was exhausted and, at the moment, she's soaking in a fragrant bath. She'll join us for dinner."

"I hope she'll abandon this silly notion of becoming a doctor," Henry said, as the brandy began to have a calming effect on him.

"Why is it a silly notion, Henry?" asked Charlotte, "I thought you were in favour of equal rights for women, or have I been married to a stranger all these years?"

"No you haven't and yes, I do," he replied. Charlotte looked at him quizzically and he added, "No, you haven't been married to a stranger and, yes, I do approve of equal rights for women."

"So, why is Letty's wish to become a doctor a silly notion?"

"Well, it is if it proves to be dangerous, like it has been today." He tapped the folded newspaper, displaying the front page headlines.

"Henry, the blame for what happened to Letty and the others today, lies clearly at the feet of those violent thugs who call themselves gentlemen and medical students," said Charlotte, her face beginning to flush, her anger towards the culprits resurfacing.

Letty entered the room just then and Henry rose and kissed his daughter on the cheek. Looking at her with concern, he asked, "How are you feeling my dear? There's a report about it in the *Evening News*."

"May I see the report please?" asked Letty, then seeing his concerned expression, she added, "yes, I'm well Father. It's just a flesh wound and will heal quickly."

He handed her the newspaper and she quickly read the report. Putting it down, she said, "That is an accurate report of the violence and hostility towards us outside the medical school, but the meeting with the Dean was very civilised," and she gave them a detailed account of the meeting in the Dean's office.

"The others are coming here tomorrow afternoon and we will discuss what we should do next."

"So, you're not giving up your quest to train as a doctor then?" her father asked, sounding very disappointed.

"No Father," Letty said, "if anything, what happened today makes me more determined than ever to become a doctor, and I wouldn't be surprised if the others feel the same."

"Well, let's go and have dinner," said Charlotte.

"Not yet Charlotte, I want this matter settled before I can eat. I'm most upset." He looked at Letty with a mixed expression of anger and pleading. "Letitia, do I have your word that this ..." he was about to say "nonsense" when his wife caught his eye with a warning look. Letty still looked mutinous. Instead he said, "Letty, do I have your word that this business of wanting to be a doctor is finished and done with?"

Her mother looked at her pleadingly and she said to him, "I give you my word that I shall take your views into consideration. I'm sorry Father, but I can't promise more than that."

Her father, sounding like he'd had all the wind knocked out of him, replied in a resigned tone, "Alright Letty, but think about what happened to you today."

"Shall we go and have dinner now?" her mother asked, and she led them out to the dining room.

That evening, Letty sat alone in her room and reflected on the uncomfortable conversation with her father. She wasn't looking forward to the possible consequences of it in the near future. She loved her father dearly but she would not let him stop her from becoming a doctor. If it was good enough for Charles and George, then she determined she would not be denied the opportunity, if, and it felt like a very big *if*, they could find a medical school who would accept them. With a heavy heart she got ready for bed.

6

THE MEETING AT LAUDER ROAD
SATURDAY 14TH MAY 1887

Letty's friends arrived together at three o'clock the next afternoon. Letty had asked Mrs Peabody, the Frobishers cook, if she would kindly bake shortbread and then she would make the tea herself, since it was Mrs Peabody's half day off.

Everything was ready in the dining room when they arrived and, as Letty showed them into the cloakroom to hang up their coats, there was a general babble of "How are you Letty dear?" or "You're looking much better than I expected!"

In response, Letty said, "Come into the dining room everyone before the tea gets cold," and she led the way through to the room which was situated at the back of the house, overlooking a mature garden where the May blossom was being blown off the branches by a keen breeze, settling the petals on the lawn like confetti.

Once they'd helped themselves to tea and shortbread from the side board, they sat around the well-polished mahogany dining table.

'Did you see the report in last night's *Evening News*?" asked Emmeline Franks.

"Yes," said Marion McNair, "and in this morning's *Scotsman*," she added, waving a copy of the paper.

Letty replied, "Yes, Father brought a copy of the *News* home with him last night and Mother sent out for the *Scotsman* this morning. That was a pretty strongly-worded editorial."

The article in the *Scotsman* was very much along the same lines as the *Evening News* of the previous day, but it came down firmly on the side of the six women. It read:

"One has to wonder at these medical students' ability to adhere to the hippocratic oath, viz. "first do no harm", when one considers the violence perpetrated by them upon unsuspecting and defenceless women. Perhaps those young men do not feel constrained to live by such ethics until the day of graduation?

One also has to wonder why those men, and the university, are so against admitting women to their medical training. Clearly, it is not because they are found wanting intellectually or academically, since they topped all the male applicants' marks in the matriculation examination. In addition to which, all of the ladies in question have already studied at Edinburgh University and excelled in the Higher Certificate in the Arts, which was the only opportunity open to them at that time and since.

What do you say boys? Is it the green-eyed monster or are you scared of being beaten by girls?"

And it went on in that vein.

"Letty, I do hope you don't mind Jessica and I speaking to the reporters after you'd gone to the hospital," said Juliette Whitton, looking a bit worried.

"Not at all Juliette," said Letty, "we didn't want to alert them beforehand in case it attracted any hostility, but as it turned out, trouble came to meet us."

"Can you believe such behaviour from the so-called better element in society?" asked Victoria Browne indignantly.

"Yes," said Jessica, "and on that point, someone made it known to those thugs that we had an appointment with the Dean."

"I suspect it was Professor Pilkington, that evil little man who spewed such vitriol in his letter to the editor of the *Scotsman* the other week," said Letty. "Well I hope they're all severely punished, including the malodorous Pilkington."

The others laughed and Marion asked, "How do you know he is smelly Letty?"

"I have inside information," she said, smiling and tapping the side of her nose in a conspiratorial manner.

"Charles!" exclaimed Victoria.

"Or George," offered Jessica.

"Or both," laughed Emmeline, "since they were both tutored by him in a confined lecture room." The women giggled.

"Seriously though," said Letty, wanting to get back to the business of the meeting, "that's all out of our hands. The question is, what do we do now?"

"Short of going abroad to train, I can't think of any way way we can get the training we want at home, or anywhere else in Britain," said a dejected Marion.

"Even if we did find a university on the Continent where we could qualify as doctors, there remains the problem of getting a licence to practice in Britain," said Juliette, adding, "and it doesn't look like that is going to happen in the near future, so it seems like we're well and truly stumped."

"Charles and Louisa came round to see me last night after hearing about what happened at the university," Letty said, thinking back to her conversation with Charles. She knew her brother well and knew that he had something up his sleeve that he wanted to share with Letty, but obviously not in their parents' hearing.

Instead, he had said, "Letty old thing, if you think you'll feel well enough, come to supper with Louisa and I tomorrow evening, won't you?"

She said now, "Actually, I think that Charles has an idea which might be helpful, but he wouldn't say anything in front of our parents. I'm going there for supper tonight and we'll be able to talk freely."

"This is beginning to feel more hopeful," said Victoria, smiling.

Letty asked them, "How did your families react on hearing about the violence and hostility yesterday?"

"Mama was furious and said I should forget about a medical degree altogether, if that's what it leads to," said Emmeline, "but I told her that it only made me more determined to train as a doctor and that I would not be cowed by thugs with inferiority complexes."

"That's just what I told my parents last night," added Letty, "but without the reference to an inferiority complex. Although I wish I had thought of it," she giggled and the others joined in with her.

The rest of them said pretty much the same thing. They were all in their mid to late twenties, so they did not need their parents permission to make such decisions, although they all agreed that it would be preferable to have their parents' blessing and funding, if they were not in possession of a legacy from deceased grandparents, or other relatives.

"That's what makes me so angry," said Marion, "I really needed that scholarship to pay for fees and living expenses."

Letty said, "Let's just concentrate on getting accepted onto a course and then we can think about where we might apply for scholarships or bursaries." They agreed and adjourned the meeting on that positive note.

7
CHARLES FINDS A SOLUTION
THAT EVENING AT HATTON PLACE

Letty walked the short distance from Lauder Road to Hatton Place to have supper with Charles and Louisa. She was very curious as to what Charles wanted to tell her. She knew it was something important, as well as exciting, since there had been a twinkle in his eye when he had invited her to supper, the previous night, in their parents' presence.

As children and young adults, this had always been a secret code between them. One would communicate to the other that he, or she, had something to say that they didn't want their parents to know about, either because they might disapprove, or that they would be told of it later.

Charles had said to come around at six-thirty if she wanted to help bathe Evangeline. Letty welcomed every opportunity of doing things for her niece as she adored the baby and had been surprised at how attached she had become to her in such a short time.

Evangeline was almost three months old and she loved her bath, splashing the water as she kicked her little legs in pleasure. At the weekend Charles usually bathed his daughter and put her to bed, since he wasn't home from work in time during the week.

He had just finished bathing Evangeline when Letty came into the nursery, a lovely little room in pastel shades.

He expertly put a clean napkin on her and dressed her in a little pink nightgown with matching bootees.

"Would you like to hold her Aunt Letty?" Charles asked, knowing well that his sister couldn't wait to hold her.

As Charles tidied away the bath things, Letty rocked Evangeline as she sang her a lullaby; it was the same one that their mother had sung to them when they were very young.

"Louisa is getting dressed for supper, she'll be along soon to kiss Evangeline goodnight and to tuck her into her cot," Charles whispered as he left the room.

Letty sang softly and watched the baby as her eyes began to close, on the threshold of sleep.

Louisa crept softly into the room and whispered, "Why don't you put her into her cot tonight Letty?"

Letty smiled and gently stood up and walked over to the cot and laid her precious bundle down with infinite care. She kissed Evangeline's forehead and whispered, "Goodnight little one, sleep well."

Louisa covered her with blankets and kissed her sleeping daughter. They stood for a few moments, gazing down at the sleeping child, then quietly left the room to join Charles downstairs in the drawing room.

Charles poured them both a dry sherry and they sat down to chat. Letty loved the Hatton Place drawing room, which was decorated in shades of blue and gold. It had a suite of comfortable chairs and a sofa in a blue and ivory stripe and the carpet was Persian, in a deep blue pattern. The marble fireplace, with the large gilt mirror above, had a fresh flower arrangement in front of the grate, as the weather was too clement for a fire.

"Well dear brother," Letty said, as she sipped her sherry, "what is all the cloak and dagger behaviour about?"

"Well sister dear," echoed Charles, "I knew Mother and Father would prefer it if you would just drop your ambition of becoming a doctor, so I thought it would be better to speak to you in their absence."

"Did they tell you that last night?"

"Apparently Father said something to Mother along the lines of you "abandoning this silly notion" and I quote."

"Oh no, Charles!" Letty was disappointed to hear this. "I wanted so much for them to continue supporting me in my quest."

"I think Mother is hoping that you will just give up the idea, after the events of yesterday."

"But I told them that the *events of yesterday*," she emphasised the words, "have only served to make me more determined to find a way of realising my dream."

"Don't give up hope Letty dear," Louisa said, "you still have our support and we shall continue to persuade Mother and Father that it is the right thing to do and that they must support you. After all, they supported Charles and George in their choice of careers."

"Thank you Louisa, but in our parents eyes that was different because they are men and George, though six years my junior, has been qualified for a number of years now." She sat in silence for some moments while she turned the crystal sherry glass around in her hands, then said, "I had a meeting this afternoon, with the others, you know, to talk about where we go from here. To think, all the elation and excitement of passing the examination has been ground into dust because of women-hating, women-fearing medical students and professors." She couldn't sit still any longer and got up and paced the room distractedly.

"We are both very sorry and angry about the shabby way you were all treated, rescinding your offer of places," said Louisa passionately, "to say nothing of the diabolical, outrageous behaviour of those louts yesterday." She then asked, "How is your head wound now Letty?"

"Oh that's fine, it's nothing really." Letty waved her hand dismissing her cut as unimportant.

"And did you come to a decision or conclusion at your meeting yesterday?" asked Charles.

"One conclusion we came to Charles, is that in order to become doctors we will have to go abroad for training, although the issue of licensing in Britain would still be a problem."

"And that is where I think I can help out Letty dear!" exclaimed Charles, grinning from ear to ear.

"I knew you had something up your sleeve Charles, I just knew it!" she said, almost dancing with excitement, "and I said as much to the girls this afternoon. Tell me all Charles dear!" demanded his sister.

"I have been giving a great deal of thought regarding you and your friends attaining a medical education, particularly in the light of the recent debate in the newspapers following your spectacular passing of the matriculation examination."

"Yes Charles, go on," replied Letty. "I'm all ears," she added, her excitement and belief that her brother had found a solution to their problem evident in her voice and sparkling eyes.

Louisa looked on with pleasure, as she knew what Charles was about to say.

"I took the liberty, I'm sure you won't mind, of corresponding with an old university friend of mine, now practising in Ireland and he informs me that the King and Queen's College of Physicians in Dublin are now taking women onto their medical training courses. He sent me a copy of their prospectus and course syllabus, along with information about making an application."

He lifted a small booklet from a side table and presented it to Letty.

She stood, open-mouthed for a moment and then she threw her arms around him and hugged him.

"So, you see Letty," said Louisa, amused and delighted for her best friend, "you will be a doctor after all." She then hugged Letty, "I'm so very happy for you."

"Let's not get carried away ladies," said Charles, "you must think it through properly. It will mean spending at least four years away from home. However, they will give you the full doctor's training that George and I got here, including practical placements on the wards of St Steeven's hospital. At the end of your training, providing you pass your final exam," he looked at his sister with smiling eyes, since he knew she would pass with honours, "you will be eligible to sit the registration examination and then you may practice anywhere in the United Kingdom."

Letty stood, hands clasped in front of her, eyes shining, "Oh Charles," she said through tears of joy, "you have made me so very happy. Thank you, thank you, dearest of all brothers."

At that moment, the gong rang for supper and they proceeded to the dining room.

"We can discuss this over supper," said Charles.

"And how to manage Mother and Father and get their support," added Louisa.

"Yes," agreed Charles, "that may be the biggest hurdle to clear now."

During supper they talked about the practicalities of how Letty and her friends, who would join her on this new course of action, should go about their applications.

"You will need testimonials, but I'm sure Wilf would be happy to provide those," said Charles.

"From his words of support and commiseration yesterday, I'm sure Professor Smithson, the Dean, would furnish me with a good testimonial."

"We seem to have covered all the practicalities, all that leaves is how to deal with Mother and Father."

They had finished supper by this time and Louisa said, rising from the table, "Why don't we have coffee in the drawing room and we can talk more comfortably there."

Charles and Letty made their way there whilst Louisa arranged for their coffee to be brought in.

"Well Charles, do you have any idea on how we should handle Mater and Pater?" asked Letty, taking the proffered coffee cup from Louisa.

"My heart tells me that you should not tell them until you have everything organised and you are sure of your acceptance on the course," said Charles, looking sheepish at the thought of deceiving his parents, even temporarily, by being complicit in the scheme, "but my head tells me that they are bound to see mail with Irish postmarks and questions will ensue."

Letty had to agree with this flaw in the plan. Then Louisa made a practical suggestion. "Why don't you put this address on your application and correspondence with the college in Dublin?"

Charles and Letty looked at each other and Letty asked, "Would you be willing to do that Charles? Could you do that, keep it all from Mother and Father like that? I really hate to be so secretive, but honestly, Father is so set against me going and relations have been rather terse lately."

Charles was in two minds, as was Letty. They were all silent for several minutes, each considering the implications and repercussions of Louisa's suggestion.

"It would be easier to tell them nearer the time, a fait accompli, if you like," Letty was the first to speak, "but is there any way they would find out, maybe from the parents of the others? Although I don't know if they mix in the same circles, apart from the Suffrage Association."

At that, they all burst into laughter for some moments, then Louisa said, "That is one very large circle!"

"Seriously," said Charles, "Mother and Father can't stop you. You are well over twenty-one," he teased her, "and you have your legacy from Grandmama, so financing your education will not be a problem."

"Thank you for reminding me of my advancing years, brother dear," she smiled, having taken no offence. "You're right, money isn't a problem for me at any rate, but poor Marion McNair was depending on the Hope Scholarship. They've been finding things difficult since her father passed away. My only difficulty might be getting Mother and Father to give me their blessing for my plans."

"Let's all take some time to think about the best way to approach our parents and we'll talk about it in a few days time," Charles replied, "It's getting late Letty, I'll walk you home."

She hugged Louisa and thanked her for a wonderful evening, promising to drop in soon.

On the walk home Charles asked his sister, "Letty dear, you're walking on air, will you be able to conceal your elation from Ma and Pa for a few days?"

"I'll try my best Charles," she replied, "I don't want to give my hand away too soon, I have so much to think about."

"In the meantime, I will try to find out if there are any charitable bodies whereby Marion may still be able to undertake the training."

"Oh Charles!" exclaimed Letty, "you are such a lovely man, thank you."

They had reached home and she kissed her brother on the cheek. "Good night and thank you for a lovely evening and such wonderful news."

She clutched the Irish prospectus in her hand and let herself into the house.

As she got ready for bed, she knew that she was far too excited to sleep.

LETTY WAS RIGHT, she could not settle to sleep. Instead, she poured over the prospectus and course syllabus from the King and Queen's College of Physicians in Ireland. (KQCPI)

The new course year was due to start on Monday 3rd of October and applications were to be submitted by the 30th of June. This gave them about six weeks to apply, in the form of a letter, as instructed. This should be sufficient time to get the required testimonials and complete the applications.

After she had read all the information and understood the timetable involved, Letty was, at last, ready to fall asleep. Just as the sun was rising, she fell into a deep restful sleep, filled with dreams of the exciting life of being a medical student.

8

THE EDINBURGH SIX
TUESDAY 17TH MAY 1887

There was a murmur of great excitement as Letty passed around cups of coffee. All five women had been able to attend the special meeting she had called.

Letty had slept late on Sunday morning and had breakfast on her own. She was glad that her parents had gone out earlier to visit relatives in the nearby countryside, since she realised she would have had difficulty hiding the excitement that kept bubbling to the surface. She felt that she must have been wearing a permanent smile, that spread from ear to ear.

After breakfast, she had cycled round to all five women. She told them briefly that there was a way to realise their dream and invited them to another meeting in Lauder Road on Tuesday, where she would share the new information that Charles had given her.

On Tuesday they were all seated around the dining table once more, notepads and pencils at the ready to write down important details.

"I told you on Saturday that I thought Charles had something up his sleeve and ..." Letty began, but was interrupted by five women all speaking at once, "Yes, you did" and "What was it?"

Letty laughed at their natural impatience and said, "Ladies, if you will give me a chance, I will tell you everything." They stopped talking and sat patiently, waiting for Letty to continue.

"Charles had heard a rumour that the King and Queen's College of Physicians in Dublin had opened its doors to women who wanted to train in medicine." She held up the prospectus and syllabus and there was a collective gasp of excitement from her audience.

"On Saturday, we reached the sad conclusion that the only way we were ever going to train as doctors was to go abroad to do so."

Emmeline spoke, "But how much more convenient to go to Ireland than the Continent. Tell us more Letty!"

"Applications to sit the entry examination must be submitted by the 30th of June and at least one testimonial, but preferably two, must be submitted with the application."

"Excellent idea!" exclaimed Victoria.

"According to the guidance, in the prospectus, I'll pass it around for you to have a look at, applications should be in the form of a letter and should include a resume of educational achievements to date and should be submitted by the 30th of June, as I mentioned earlier."

"So far, so good." said Jessica.

Letty continued, "Letters of recommendation, or testimonials, should be included with your application.

"Who will furnish us with a testimonial?" asked a fretful Marion.

"Don't look so worried Marion," said Letty encouragingly, "we can ask Dr Cunningham and Professor Smithson."

"Professor Smithson?" she asked, "but he turned us down."

"No Marion," replied Letty, "to be fair, he didn't turn us down. Remember he said he was in favour of us being admitted?"

Seeing the light at the end of, what for her was a long dark tunnel, Marion brightened somewhat. "Yes he did, didn't he?"

"Do you think Dr Cunningham would be willing to write one for each of us?" asked Juliette.

"I'm sure he would," replied Letty, "but remember how sympathetic Professor Smithson was last Friday?" They all nodded. "I think we should ask him to write us a testimonial too, it may ease his conscience somewhat, after our ordeal at the hands of his students."

Letty read from the prospectus, "The entrance examination is being held on the 1st of August and successful candidates will be notified shortly after the 8th of August."

A thought suddenly struck her and she said, "Wait! Perhaps if Professor Smithson sends them our results then they might waive the necessity of us sitting another exam."

"Well, that would indeed be a blessing." said Emmeline.

They were all thoughtful for a while, contemplating the task ahead of them and then the practicalities of studying and living in an another country.

"It means we will have to pay for accommodation," said Jessica, "and I was relying on living at home, free of charge."

"Since there is no possibility of us studying at Edinburgh University, then we would have to pay for accommodation, whether in Ireland or on the Continent," said Emmeline.

"That's very true," said Marion, looking despondent again.

"What's bothering you Marion?" asked Letty, thinking she already knew what the problem was.

"It's just this whole awful business of finding the money for the course. With rescinding our places, we were also deprived of the Hope Scholarship."

"If it's any consolation," said Victoria, "I'm in pretty much the same position as you."

Letty interjected, "Charles is trying to find out if there are any charitable bodies or philanthropic societies that you could apply to for financial assistance." There were murmurs of surprised interest among the group.

Then Jessica said, "I don't mean to sound like the voice of doom, but any that exist would probably only sponsor men, and women may not be eligible to even apply."

"Which would be logical," said Juliette, "since we can't even get into a British University to study."

Emmeline said, "Let's not give up hope, let's be positive until we are told something to the contrary."

"Jolly well said!" added Jessica.

"Now, a bit of a thorny problem has arisen for me," said Letty.

They all looked in surprise at the usually confident, self-possessed Letitia Frobisher.

"I'm not sure how my parents will react when I tell them I'm going to Ireland to study medicine. Have any of you told your parents about the possibility of having to go abroad?"

They all looked sheepish and Victoria said, "Actually, I haven't mentioned it to mine either. I didn't want to risk another diatribe on how abominably young men in universities treat ladies and how I'm better to be well out of it etc etc."

Letty looked at Emmeline, Juliette, Marion, Victoria and Jessica in turn and they all replied, "Same here."

"I suppose," said Jessica, "it would be a wee bit premature mentioning it to our parents in case the whole thing falls through."

"I agree," said Victoria, "once we have an invitation to sit the examination will be time enough to tell them."

"Alright then, this is what I propose," announced Letty, "time is of the essence and I suggest we all sit here and write our letters of application. Once we have done that, we will write to Dr Cunningham and Professor Smithson. Does everyone have enough time to stay here and do that?"

They all agreed they had.

"I will hand-deliver our letters to Dr Cunningham and I will ask Charles to deliver the ones to the Professor. I'm reluctant to leave anything to chance after our meeting with him was made known to the students."

"Hear! Hear!" agreed Juliette.

"Right then," said Letty, "I will fetch paper, ink and pens from Mother's study."

AN HOUR AND A HALF LATER, after various false starts and screwed up sheets of paper, all the letters had been written and envelopes addressed. Everyone thought it best that the letters of application should be held by Letty until the testimonials had been received.

The five women left the house in Lauder Road in high spirits and Letty waved them off. There was just one more thing that she had to do, and that was to arrange a private meeting with Professor Smithson, but this time, it would be well away from the Medical School. She smiled to herself, satisfied with a morning's work well done.

9

THAT AFTERNOON

Later that afternoon, Letty cycled to Dr Cunningham's home in Salisbury Place and put all six letters through the letterbox. She then cycled to Hatton Place with the letters for Professor Smithson.

Gertie, the maid, opened the door to her. She said "The mistress is in the drawing room Miss Frobisher, shall I announce you?"

"No Gertie, I'll just go straight through.

Louisa looked up from the book she was reading when Letty entered the room. "Letty, it's lovely to see you," said Louisa, getting up and giving her sister-in-law a hug.

"Letty looked at Louisa keenly and asked, "Are you feeling alright Louisa? You look rather pale."

"I'm fine," she replied, "having a baby in the house is quite tiring, even with a nurse for Evangeline. If she cries during the night, I tend to get up even though I know Mary has the situation in hand."

"Do you think you have fully recovered from the birth? You do look very tired," then Letty said thoughtfully. "I didn't notice on Saturday evening because I was so excited by the news Charles gave me."

"Stop fretting Letty," Louisa replied, "I am well. Your brother would notice right away if there was anything amiss."

"Of course, you're right, I'm just being silly."

"Have you come round on a social visit or are you on "medical education" business?" She eyed the large envelope in Letty's hand.

"A bit of both actually," Letty said and sat down on the sofa.

"Would you like some tea?"

"No, thank you, I won't be staying long, but you have some if you want."

"No, I won't, I had some a little while ago. What's your business reason for the visit?" Louisa asked, curious to know what was in the envelope.

"It might sound unlikely but I don't trust the staff at the Medical School after what happened last Friday and I thought I would write to Professor Smithson and ask him to meet me at a venue away from the university."

"Yes, I see," said Louisa, "at least I think I do."

"Would you and Charles mind awfully if that venue were to be here?" Letty asked a trifle nervously.

"I certainly don't mind and I can't think of any reason why Charles would object," replied Louisa, "we'll do everything in our power to further your wish to study medicine. You can use Charles's study for the meeting, that is, if the Professor agrees to meet you."

"Oh thank you Louisa, thank you so much," said Letty, feeling very relieved. "You see, I want to ask him personally if he would be willing to provide testimonials for the *Edinburgh Six* and ..."

Louisa interrupted her, "The what? What's the Edinburgh Six?"

Letty reminded her of the Edinburgh Seven in 1870, the violence towards those women had been widely publicised in the newspapers at that time.

"Of course, how could I forget such diabolical behaviour towards them."

"Yes," agreed Letty, "last Friday was like history repeating itself. But, as I was saying, I want to explain to the professor what we are hoping to do and also to ask him if he will include the results of our Matriculation examination last month. You see we're asking the college in Dublin if they will waive the entrance examination for us in the light of evidence of the Edinburgh exams. We will take the examination if we have to, but we would rather save ourselves the journey, and the added expense for one or two of the others."

"I see," said Louisa, "but wouldn't they think you're not very serious about the training if you sound as though you are trying to get out of the examination?"

"That's a good point Louisa. Yes, we'll leave it to them to waive the examination requirement, or not."

"Yes, I think that would be better. You don't want to be accused of being the *Edinburgh Viragos*," Louisa smiled at her. "Are you going to tell me what's in that envelope, or will you wait until I burst with curiosity?"

Letty looked at her lap and realised she was still clutching the envelope containing the letters of application.

She laughed and explained what they were, frowned, then said after a moment's thought, "I was going to ask if I could leave them here, but I will now have to go back to the others and get them to rewrite them, leaving out the part where we ask for the exam to be waived," she smiled ruefully, "still, time is on our side at this stage." She stood up ready to leave and Louisa asked, "Would you like to see Evangeline before you go?"

"I was just about to ask, yes please, that would be lovely."

After looking in on her beautiful godchild, Letty cycled home, happy in the knowledge that the first step towards gaining a place at the Dublin college was in progress.

WILLIAM JOSEPH SMITHSON was only too happy to oblige Miss Frobisher. He responded by return of post and suggested a time and date. He was secretly intrigued by the six women who had come to his office, particularly Miss Frobisher who had been their spokesperson.

He had been truthful when he said he was in favour of allowing women to train as doctors and to his chagrin, that Friday morning, he thought he would never hear of, or from, them again. He genuinely wished them well and felt ashamed of the university's archaic stand on not allowing women to study for degrees generally, but especially when it came to medicine.

He could not believe Pilkington, when he claimed the women he asked said they did not want female doctors. He also suspected his colleague of being behind the attack on the women, but so far, no one was opening up when questioned. They had closed ranks and he hoped that the police investigation would get further than the university's own half-hearted attempt.

Therefore, it transpired that, a week later, Professor Smithson met Letty at Louisa and Charles's house. The professor was aware of the Consultant Paediatrician by reputation, but he had not realised the connection between Miss Frobisher and Dr Frobisher.

Louisa's housekeeper brought them a pot of coffee and home-made shortbread, which was still warm from the oven and smelled delicious.

Once Letty had poured the coffee and offered the Dean some shortbread, she said, "First of all, thank you for agreeing to meet with me. You must be wondering why all the 'cloak and dagger' business."

"Not at all, Miss Frobisher. I can understand very well why you would prefer not to come anywhere near the medical school after what happened on the thirteenth. How can I be of assistance to you?"

Letty explained about applying to the college in Dublin and the request for two testimonials.

"Dr Cunningham has kindly agreed to provide us each with one and, although one might do, two is their preference, especially when one would be from the Medical School at Edinburgh University, who had accepted us at one time."

"Quite," Professor Smithson said, still feeling shame at the way the university had treated these women. "I am very happy to write testimonials for all of you. I will also include your matriculation examination results from Edinburgh and, with luck, they may waive the need for you all to make the journey there to sit their own examination. I think most entrance examinations for medical degrees are more or less standardised now."

"Thank you Professor, we are very grateful to you."

"It's the least I can do Miss Frobisher, to compensate for the extremely shabby way that the university has treated you."

"You have shown us nothing but kindness and respect Professor, and we appreciate that," said Letty.

"You will all be in receipt of your testimonial letters by the end of the week. I wish you all the very best and, perhaps, you would let me know how you all fare with your applications?"

"I will keep you informed of our progress Professor," replied Letty.

"You never know, Miss Frobisher, perhaps one, or more, of your cohort will one day be lecturers at the Medical School," said the Dean, "we can all hope for such progress in the course of time." He stood up to leave. "It has been a pleasure to meet with you again Miss Frobisher."

"And you, Professor Smithson, and thank you again for agreeing to help us. We are fortunate to have you and Dr Cunningham as allies." She saw him to the door and then hurried to tell Louisa the good news.

As soon as the meeting with the Dean had been confirmed, Letty had arranged a meeting with the others for that afternoon. Now she could hardly wait to tell them the good news. "We are finally on our way to a medical degree," she thought with much pleasure.

10

SATURDAY, 4TH JUNE

Since the birth of their daughter, Charles had always been very solicitous of Louisa's health and well-being, more so than most husbands, and it was due, in the main, to the fact that he had almost lost Louisa eighteen months previously.

In the course of her work with neglected and abused children in Edinburgh, it had been her misfortune to unwittingly stumble upon an illicit trade in young girls. This subsequently led to Louisa's life and virtue being put at great risk.

One sunny day in October 1885, whilst taking Harvey, Louisa's greyhound-deerhound cross, for a walk, she was kidnapped and Harvey, who had tried to protect his mistress, was left for dead.

The revengeful George Galbraith, brothel owner and procurer of young girls, had ordered her abduction and had been planning a particularly cruel revenge on Louisa. Fortunately for Louisa, the police raided Galbraith's premises at 42 Royal Terrace, and arrested several prominent members of Edinburgh Society, caught in *flagrante delicto*.

A thorough search of the place failed to find Louisa. However, during the questioning of the premises' housekeeper the next day, she told the police of the existence of a second, or lower, basement and Louisa was found, unharmed.

Galbraith's men had used chloroform to render her unconscious and the memory of the nausea and headaches was still very fresh, hence Louisa's refusal to have it when giving birth to Evangeline.

Evangeline was now almost three months old and beginning to take notice of her surroundings and those who peopled it. She particularly loved Harvey, and would try to grab his hairy eyebrows or ears.

Louisa enjoyed taking her daughter for walks in her perambulator, risking the disapproval of some of her neighbours. As a rule, women of her class did not do that, that was the job of the nanny.

Charles and Louisa were unusual in this respect and defied the social niceties. They were often seen walking around the Hermitage of Braid, near Blackford Hill. Even though Evangeline was too young to understand, Charles would point out the trees and birds and squirrels on their trips out. She seemed to be delighted by it all and would gurgle away happily. Harvey always accompanied them, as the self-appointed protector of the baby girl.

The little family had just returned from such an outing and Charles said, "I'm just going to the hospital for last ward rounds, I shouldn't be more than an hour."

"I'll let Mrs Hammond know before taking Evangeline to the nursery for her supper. Then I may have a rest until you return. Goodbye Charles," Louisa said, kissing him lightly on the cheek.

Louisa liked to give Evangeline her supper before Mary

bathed her and put her down to sleep for the night. If she was feeling tired, as she did now after their walk, Mary would do it.

Louisa hadn't fully recovered her strength since Evangeline's birth and she felt fatigued a lot of the time. This fact, she was careful to conceal from Charles, as she didn't want him fussing over her.

After her tea and bath, Mary brought Evangeline in to say goodnight to Louisa. She breathed in her sweet baby scent as she cuddled her and kissed her goodnight.

Louisa changed her mind about having a rest and decided to get on with the arrangements for a small dinner party, planned for the 18th of June, which was to be in honour of their first wedding anniversary and Louisa's 29th birthday.

She went into her study and sat at her desk with pen and paper. This would keep her occupied until Charles returned. The study was at the back of the house, overlooking the south-facing garden. It was comfortably furnished with a well-polished mahogany desk; pens and ink sat in a silver holder in front of the large blotting pad.

The desk chair was of soft leather and made a lengthy stint at the desk comfortable. There were also two comfortable easy chairs, placed either side of the fireplace and the walls were decorated with a pale gold wallpaper which gave the room a sunny ambience, even on rainy days. The deep blue of the carpet matched the velvet curtains and gave the room an air of calm which encouraged thought.

She had just made a list of guests who would be invited and was thinking about the menu when she suddenly felt unwell. She shook her head, trying to dispel the strange feeling that had come over her, when she was doubled over by an agonising pain that mercilessly gripped her abdomen like a vice. The pain was so all-consuming that she struggled to breathe. She took a few deep breaths and rose from the chair to ring the bell by the fireplace but she did not reach it. She collapsed onto the floor, unconscious.

Harvey, who had followed her into the study, had begun to whimper feebly as he sensed his mistress's distress. His whimpering became howls as Louisa fell to the floor and this brought Mrs Hammond, running from the kitchen in the direction of Harvey's wails.

On entering the study, she saw Louisa on the floor with an anxious Harvey standing guard over her and blood pouring onto the floor from under her skirt.

The housekeeper checked Louisa was still breathing then coaxed Harvey into the kitchen where Gertie was preparing the vegetables for supper.

"Gertie," said Mrs Hammond, "run along tae the hospital as fast as ye can an' get Dr Frobisher. Mrs Frobisher is very ill, tell him."

Gertie hesitated, confused, as she had seen Mrs Frobisher just half an hour before and she was fine. "Run Gertie, now!" shouted Mrs Hammond, which galvanised Gertie into action.

Mary, who had just got Evangeline off to sleep ran out onto the upstairs landing to see what all the commotion and barking was about. Miraculously, Harvey's howling had not disturbed the baby.

The housekeeper called up to her, "Mary come down quick and stay wi' the Mistress while Ah run across the road an' see if Dr Henderson is hame yet." Satisfied that Mary was on her way downstairs, she flew out of the house and across the road to "Hillview", the doctor's residence.

Fortunately, Dr Henderson was just returning from his general practice in Morningside and his driver was about to drive round to the mews to stable his horse for the night. Mrs Hammond's calls stopped both men in their tracks. She quickly told the doctor about Mrs Frobisher and he followed her back across the road.

Mary, a trained nurse, had taken Louisa's pulse when she went into the study. She looked worried by the amount of blood Louisa was losing. Harvey, who had been shut in the kitchen was still whimpering, but more softly and resignedly now.

Mary said, "Her pulse is getting weaker doctor and I don't like how pale she is. Dr Frobisher has been sent for."

Dr Henderson took one look at Louisa's deathly pale face and said, "She's haemorrhaging, get some towels quickly."

Mary ran to the linen cupboard and returned in seconds with thick bath towels which the doctor used to try to stem the relentless flow of blood.

Charles entered the room just as Dr Henderson said, "We'll have to get her to the hospital right away, she's lost a lot of blood."

Charles looked at his beloved Louisa, lying so still. He asked, "What's her pulse rate David?"

His neighbour replied, "It's very slow and very faint, I'm afraid Charles. It's imperative we get her to the hospital now. I have my carriage ready to take us."

Charles nodded dumbly. This is what he had been afraid of, ever since Evangeline was born. He was well aware that it could happen at any time, sometimes months after giving birth, and was the cause of many maternal deaths.

It was important to keep her warm to prevent her body going into shock and Charles wrapped Louisa up warmly in soft blankets that Mary had brought when she knew her mistress would be going to the hospital. He carried her, as gently as possible, into the doctor's waiting carriage. The journey to the Royal Infirmary felt endless to Charles, although in reality, it took just over ten minutes.

At the hospital, Louisa was put onto a trolley and quickly taken to the gynaecology ward. A porter had been sent on ahead to let them know a consultant was required for a dangerously ill patient.

As soon as they reached the ward, Louisa was whisked away to the operating theatre whilst Dr Henderson gave his report to the consultant. Charles was asked to wait outside in the waiting room, or to go to the doctors lounge since he was a well-known doctor in his own right.

Dr Henderson had offered to wait with Charles, but Charles told him to go home to his family and his supper, with his immense gratitude.

"Thank you David and bless you for being on hand. I can't bear to think of the consequences if you hadn't arrived home at that moment."

Dr Henderson said, "It's that big dog of yours you should thank. From what I gathered, he sent up an almighty howling that brought your housekeeper to Louisa right away. But for Harvey, I think your dear wife may have bled to death on the study floor."

Charles shook his hand and, with tears in his eyes, said in a hoarse voice, "Bless you David and God bless our faithful Harvey." Then he reluctantly went to the waiting room which, mercifully was empty at this time of the evening. He paced to and fro for what felt like hours and was about to go to the theatre and make enquiries when Sir James Young Simpson, the consultant gynaecologist, entered the waiting room.

"How is she Sir?" asked Charles, without waiting for the man to speak.

Sit down Dr Frobisher," he said, sitting down himself. Charles sat down, anxious to hear what the other man had to tell him.

"The haemorrhage was caused by a small area of the placenta that had not come away with the afterbirth and which had adhered to the uterus."

"I have worried since our daughter was born that Louisa wasn't right and I had thought Sister McNally had delivered the placenta intact," Charles said, feeling guilty.

"These things happen, as you well know and I can assure you, there was no negligence involved. Giving birth is a hazardous business."

"But will Louisa be alright? She will survive, won't she?"

"Your wife's condition is stable, but she has lost a lot of blood. We have put her on a saline solution which I hope will lead to a full recovery, but I must warn you, the next few hours are crucial and she is being given the best care possible."

"What about a blood transfusion, with me as donor? Blundell did it decades ago." asked Charles, desperate not to lose his darling Louisa.

"Let us see how the saline works first before considering performing a potentially risky procedure." He looked at Charles's ravaged face and softened his tone. "I'm not sure it would work Dr Frobisher, it hasn't been attempted much since Blundell tried it in 1813. There are too many imponderables, including blood types and getting a suitable match. Research still has a long way to go, I'm afraid."

"Will she die without a transfusion of blood?" asked Charles.

Sir James kept his steady gaze on Charles and said, "Possibly, but equally possibly, a transfusion may kill her." He laid his hand on Charles's shoulder and said, "Let us try the saline infusion first and then we'll see."

Reluctantly, Charles had to agree, "May I see her please Sir James?"

"Of course, you know the way. I'll be on call if needed," then he added, "remember to scrub up first." as if Charles needed to be told to do that.

Charles entered the single room where Louisa was being cared for. A nurse was sitting by the bed monitoring the infusion and she looked up and smiled as he approached the bed.

He looked at Louisa who seemed so pale and fragile on the white pillows and the white counterpane. Her beautiful auburn hair seemed to intensify her fragility by its rich and lively colour.

"Sit here," the nurse said, "I'll get another chair as I have to watch the drip and change it when it's time."

"Thank you," said Charles and he sat down and put his hand over Louisa's, which were lying on the bedcover.

"I'll leave you to have a little privacy with Mrs Frobisher since the saline still has some time to run. But call for me if you need me, I'll be at the nurses station in the big ward."

Charles nodded and the nurse left the room. He looked at Louisa, "Louisa, it's Charles. You must get better my darling. I love you so much Louisa, please get better for my sake and little Evangeline."

He stayed like this by Louisa's side, waiting, hoping, praying for a miracle.

He was still praying when the nurse returned with another chair and she could see his face was wet with tears. She asked him, "Dr Frobisher, would you like to make yourself a hot drink in the ward kitchen?"

"Thank you for the offer Nurse ...?" he realised he didn't know her name.

"Nurse Dean, Dr Frobisher"

"Yes, thank you for the offer Nurse Dean, but I'd rather just sit here by my wife's side, if that's alright."

"That's alright doctor," she replied and smiled reassuringly at him.

The long night wore on with no sign of Louisa regaining consciousness and still Charles sat, holding her hand.

11

EDINBURGH ROYAL INFIRMARY
EARLY SUNDAY MORNING

Dawn breaks early in June and Charles awoke as the light flooded into the little room. He was sitting slumped over in his chair with his head on the bed and he had a crick in his neck.

His first reaction was to look at Louisa, who lay still and pale. Nurse Dean, who was sitting in the corner and whose presence he had been unaware of on wakening, spoke, "Mrs Frobisher has had two more infusions during the night and her condition is stable, though still unconscious, as you can see Dr Frobisher."

She had stood up and was taking Louisa's pulse. When she had made a note on the chart, she said, "Sir James will look in around seven o'clock on his first ward rounds."

Charles thought that Louisa looked less pale than when she came out of the theatre and her breathing was steady.

Nurse Dean regarded the haggard-looking man with sympathy and said, "Dr Frobisher, why don't you go home and sleep for a couple of hours and come back after Sir James's rounds? You know, your wife couldn't be in better hands than Sir James Simpson's."

Sir James was the son of Sir James Young Simpson, who pioneered the use of chloroform to ease the pain of childbirth and who the new purpose-built maternity hospital was named after. Sir James, the younger, was a highly respected gynaecologist and obstetrician.

Charles looked at Louisa again, trying to decide on whether to remain by her side or to go home, then having made the decision, he reluctantly agreed.

IT WAS JUST after five o'clock when he got out of the hansom cab and paid the driver. He walked slowly up the path of 4 Hatton Place, unaware of the early morning scents from the garden, or the birdsong. He let himself quietly into the house, not wanting to disturb the the sleeping household.

Harvey came bounding up the hallway as soon as he heard Charles's key in the lock, tail wagging, then he looked confused as he realised that Louisa was not with him. Charles bent to stroke the the shaggy, grey head and rubbed Harvey's ears. He said, "If God answers our prayers Harvey, your mistress will be home soon. Now go and lie on your bed, there's a good boy."

When Charles entered the kitchen, the members of the household were already up and about their duties, having been unable to sleep. On seeing him, Mrs Hammond put the kettle on for tea.

She asked, "How is the mistress Dr Frobisher? Dr Henderson kindly came in last night, when he returned from the Infirmary, and told us Mrs Frobisher was in the operating theatre."

Charles sat down wearily on a chair at the solid kitchen table and said, "Still unconscious, I'm afraid, but she's in a stable condition and in good hands, under the care of Sir James Simpson."

"We've a' been prayin' for her Sir and will continue to do so. Now can Ah get ye some breakfast? Ye'll need tae keep yer strength up," said the housekeeper kindly.

"That's kind of you, Mrs Hammond, just tea please and then I'll get an hour or two of sleep, after I look in on Evangeline. I'll be going back to the hospital after their morning rounds."

"Right ye are Sir," said Mrs Hammond, as she poured boiling water over the tea leaves in the warming teapot.

The kitchen in Hatton Place was a sunny room with pale yellow walls and a well-polished oak floor. The large window overlooked the south-facing back garden and the soft early morning sun poured into the room, burnishing the copper pots and pans which hung from a pulley.

Charles looked around the kitchen, then, cup and saucer in hand, walked over to the window. He looked out at the mature garden with its fruit and vegetable beds. None of it seemed familiar, nothing felt familiar while his precious wife lay between life and death.

He vowed there and then, that if Louisa recovered, "and she must recover," he thought to himself, there would be no more children and no more risk to her life. Much as he cherished their lovemaking, he loved his wife more. Louisa's life was of paramount importance. "We'll just have to find closeness in other ways, I cannot and will not put her life at risk again." His decision was final.

He thought back to their wedding and honeymoon, almost one year ago, and how they had happily planned to have several children. Louisa said she'd had a very solitary childhood and wanted their son or daughter to have siblings.

Then his mind went back to Louisa's labour three months earlier and how careful he had been in choosing a good midwife for her. He had insisted on Sister McNally having a freshly laundered uniform and the scrubbing of hands with carbolic soap. He knew the risk of Puerperal Pyrexia, an infection of the womb which had been a killer of women for centuries. This infection had been spread from patient to patient by doctors and midwives who carried it on their hands and clothes, ignorant of the infection they were passing from woman to woman. Doctors and professors of medicine had rejected this idea for many years, vilifying proponents of using antiseptics, such as carbolic soap.

It was no mere catastrophic thinking on Charles's part, since he knew only too well how heavy the maternal death toll was.

He gave himself a mental shake as Mrs Hammond's bustling around the kitchen brought him back to the present. She was a treasure and the sister of Lady Moncrieff's housekeeper. She was a sturdy, motherly woman in her late forties and she adored her mistress of twelve months as much as her constant companion, Harvey, and was often found giving him scraps in the kitchen on the quiet.

Charles said, "Thank you for the tea Mrs Hammond, it hit the spot right enough." He smiled at her but she could see the sadness and worry behind his attempts at cheerfulness. "I'll go on up to the nursery now."

"Good morning Mary," he said, on entering. It was an airy room with pictures of rabbits, ducks and hens on the wall. The wallpaper was patterned with rainbows, fluffy white clouds and baby animals on a blue background.

"Good morning Dr Frobisher, may I ask how Mrs Frobisher is?" She was in the process of dressing Evangeline, having just given her breakfast.

"Still unconscious, I'm afraid Mary, but stable, they tell me. They operated and managed to stop the bleeding, she is having saline infusions to help replenish the blood she has lost."

"I've been praying for a full recovery, we all have Sir."

Evangeline was smiling and gurgling happily, blissfully unaware of the danger her mother was in. "Would you like to hold Evangeline for a little while?" Mary asked.

"Just for five minutes Mary, I have to get a couple of hours sleep and then get back to the hospital."

She handed the baby to her father. He took his daughter in his arms and she looked up at him. Her eyes were the same shade of blue as her mother's. Her face broke into a wide, gummy smile as he cradled her in his arms.

He walked around the room with her, pointing to the little stuffed animal toys and showing her the baby animals on the wallpaper.

Presently, feeling the heavy burden of all that had transpired in the past twelve hours, "Was it only twelve hours?" he asked himself. He said to Mary, "Take her now Mary and would you please ask Mrs Hammond to bring me tea and hot water at eight-thirty."

Putting Evangeline in her white cot, above which blue angel shapes dangled and moved around on a mobile, Mary replied, "Of course, Dr Frobisher. I hope you have a refreshing sleep."

In the bedroom he had shared with Louisa for almost a year, he undressed wearily and got into bed. The bed felt too big and empty without Louisa. He worried that he would be too tired to sleep, with the unrelenting emotions of the long hours at the hospital but, as he lay breathing in Louisa's scent from her pillows, he fell into a restful and mercifully, dreamless slumber.

12

LATER THAT MORNING

Back at the hospital, Charles went directly to see Louisa, deciding to leave talking to Sir James until after he had made his own assessment of Louisa's condition.

On entering Louisa's room, he noticed that there was some colour in her cheeks and hope stirred in his heart.

"How is she?" he asked the nurse, a different one from the previous night. "I'm Dr Frobisher, Louisa's husband," he added, approaching the bed, "I see she has some colour in her cheeks," then he stopped short and his heart sank again as he saw how hot Louisa was.

He looked questioningly at the nurse, who said, "Sir James was here earlier and has asked that you go to his office as soon as you arrived Dr Frobisher."

It was then that he noticed she was wringing out a cloth from a bowl of cold water and applying it to Louisa's forehead.

"She has a fever then?" Charles asked, although he knew the answer to this question. He turned around and made his way along the labyrinth of corridors in the hospital until he reached the consultant's office. He knocked on the door, feeling his anxiety increase with every second that passed.

"Come in!" said a disembodied voice from within.

Charles entered the office, surprisingly sparsely furnished for a man of his exalted position.

"Ah, Dr Frobisher, please sit down," said the other man.

"My wife has a fever Sir James, is the saline not effective?"

"It's still too early to tell, as there can be a delayed response to the infusion. And yes, she developed a fever around two hours ago, as you will have noticed, we are trying to reduce it and make her comfortable."

"How much danger is she in?" asked Charles, but fearing the reply.

"At this moment in time, I would put your wife's chance of recovery at thirty percent. Now, you know as well as I do, that it can change either way."

"What about a transfusion? Perhaps if we had done that last night when I suggested it, my wife might not be lying there with a thirty percent chance of recovery." Charles sounded angry as his frustration at the man's reticence escaped his weakening control of his emotions.

He added, "Damn it man, if it was your wife, how would you feel?"

"As I said last night Dr Frobisher, a blood transfusion carries a substantial risk. Mrs Frobisher's body is struggling as it is and I don't want to overload her system further." said the consultant with surprising patience and empathy.

Charles relented immediately and said, "I do apologise for my outburst Sir James, I am overwrought and cannot bear to think of losing my wife."

Before leaving for the hospital, he had asked Gertie to take a cab to Heriot Row with a note informing Louisa's parents of the situation. It said they could make a brief visit in the afternoon. He now worried whether they would find their only daughter alive. A similar note was taken by Mrs Hammond to his own parents nearby.

"Come along Charles," said Sir James, bringing him back from his grim thoughts, "let us go and see your wife."

Louisa had become restive, during Charles's absence and she was calling for him. He was at her side in a moment. "Thank God you're back Louisa," he said, tears welling up.

The nurse informed them that Louisa had regained consciousness only a few moments earlier and had been about to send for them when they entered the room.

"She is still far from well Dr Frobisher," said the consultant, taking Louisa's pulse and putting his hand on her feverish brow.

He instructed the nurse, "We must discontinue the saline infusions Nurse Wilson, and get me five drops of laudanum in three ounces of water." As he removed the drip, he said to Charles, "If this amount of saline is not effective, there is no point in giving her any more."

Charles looked on helpless as the nurse returned with the glass of medicine. Sir James said, "You give it to her Charles and stay as long as you wish. I'll look in again later." Turning to Nurse Wilson, he said, "Repeat the same dose of laudanum every four hours please," and he left the room.

All that day, Louisa slipped in and out of consciousness, at times sleeping peacefully, whilst at other times she thrashed about the bed and ranted deliriously, calling for Charles, Evangeline and even Harvey.

At one point the nurse sent Charles to get something to eat and drink while she gave Louisa a bed bath, in the hope of reducing her fever.

Lord and Lady Moncrieff, Louisa's parents, visited in the

afternoon and stayed only a short time as it was extremely distressing to see their daughter so grievously ill.

"Oh Charles," Lady Moncrieff cried, "I thought our worries about Louisa were over when she was rescued from that awful basement in Royal Terrace." Her husband put his arm around her shoulders and drew her to him, trying to comfort her. "Come Emily," he said, on the verge of tears himself, "let us kiss Louisa and go home. All we can do now is wait and pray that she recovers."

Letty came in to see Louisa around four o'clock. She sat with Charles and watched powerless, as the fever raged. "My poor Louisa," said Letty, as she gently stroked Louisa's cheek, tears falling from her eyes. "Charles, this makes me more determined than ever to be a doctor. There isn't enough being done to protect women from the risks of childbirth. Even with you and a good midwife, there are still hidden risks."

"I know Letty." Charles face looked ravaged with worry and grief, "All we can do now is hope and pray that our darling Louisa survives. I can't bear to think of losing her or of Evangeline growing up without her mother, or knowing what a good, kind woman she is." He bowed his head and tears fell down his face and dropped onto his hands, folded in his lap.

"Charles," Letty said, "I won't let you go down that way of thinking. We must believe Louisa will recover. We must." She was weeping too.

They sat in silence for some time, then Letty stood up and kissed her friend. "Louisa," she whispered, "you must get better for the sake of your daughter. I'll be back tomorrow to see you." She hugged Charles and left the sick room.

Sir James looked in again at around seven-thirty and he

examined Louisa. "I should say that it's just a matter of a few hours until the fever reaches its peak," he told Charles, "and then we can only pray that it breaks."

Charles, who no longer had any words, nodded and continued his vigil as Nurse Dean returned to do her night shift. She continued with the four hourly medication and the cold compresses.

As the hours ticked slowly by, Charles was mentally preparing himself for the worst and was in the depths of despair. Suddenly, he heard Louisa say his name. He had been sitting with his elbows on his knees and his head in his hands, but he shot up out of the chair, hoping he wasn't dreaming.

"Charles," she said again in a hoarse whisper, "I'm thirsty, may I have some water please."

Both Charles and Nurse Dean studied Louisa closely and smiled to each other with monumental relief, this was no feverish raving, as before, Louisa's eyes were clear.

While the nurse went to fetch Sir James, Charles poured water into a glass and helped Louisa to drink. He checked her pulse which was strong and steady, and said, "Welcome back my darling Louisa. I am so happy and relieved that I don't know whether to to laugh or cry.."

Just then, Sir James entered the room with Nurse Dean. He said, "Welcome back my dear Mrs Frobisher! You are made of strong stuff dear lady." He examined her and was satisfied that she was indeed recovering. He asked, "Do you think you could manage some clear soup?"

"I think so," Louisa replied.

"And then, you must get a good night's sleep. You'll feel much better in the morning." He left the room saying, "I'll be back to see you in the morning, goodnight Mrs Frobisher and well done!"

A little while later, after Louisa managed to take some soup, Charles kissed his wife and said, "Goodnight Louisa, sleep well and I shall see you in the morning. I shall go directly to your parents and let them know that you are recovering and should be home in a few days."

"Thank you Charles, they will appreciate that." She yawned, "goodnight Charles" she said sleepily.

By ten-thirty that night, Charles had seen both Louisa's and his own parents and told them the wonderful news about Louisa. That night, he went to bed and slept a deep, untroubled sleep. Even Harvey was more at peace, he seemed to understand that everything was going to be alright.

13
RED LETTER DAY
21ST JULY 1887

It transpired that all six women who had applied to the King and Queen's College of Physicians in Ireland, were offered places.

On the strength of the testimonials submitted by Dr Cunningham and Professor Smithson, it was decided that they would not be required to sit another entrance examination. The professor had furnished them with sufficient information that the Irish college was satisfied that they were suitably qualified for admission to the medical degree course.

When Letty came downstairs for breakfast, she picked up the mail which had been left on the hall table. She quickly sifted through the various letters, as she had done every day for the past few weeks.

She stopped suddenly when she saw the Irish postmark and she knew that this was the moment of truth. With shaking hands, she pried the letter open and began to read its contents. It read:

"Dear Miss Frobisher,

Re: Medical Degree Application

I am writing to inform you that your application for admission to the above named course has been successful."

She did not need to read any further. "Yes!" she exclaimed, "Oh my goodness, I'm going to be a doctor!" She ran into the breakfast room where her mother was just finishing her breakfast and said in a rush, "Look Mother," proffering her the letter, "I've been accepted, can you believe it? Isn't it the most wonderful news ever?"

"Congratulations Letty dear," her mother said, "you deserve some good news at last, but I dread to think how your father will react to this news."

One week earlier

LETTY HAD FINALLY TOLD THEM, with Charles there for moral support, that she and her friends had applied to train as doctors in Dublin.

"But Letty," her mother had lamented, "look what happened to you in Edinburgh. I really don't want you putting yourself at risk in another country."

Her father had agreed with her mother, "Your mother is right Letty and I agree that you'll be better off staying at home and thinking about a different career."

Letty was on the verge of tears when Charles intervened. He said, "Mother, Father, the medical college in Dublin has been allowing women to take its licensing examination for the past decade and for the past two years have been admitting women on their medical degree courses." Their parents were listening with interest and he continued, "The attitude towards female medical students and doctors is not like that in the University of Edinburgh, where they seem intent on keeping their doors closed to women. On the contrary, women are welcomed on the course there and in the teaching hospitals. Edinburgh Royal Infirmary refused to accommodate women on its wards for their practical training, citing it as another legitimate - in their eyes - reason for barring them from the training."

"Oh I see," said his mother, still a little unsure. His father remained silent.

Letty said, "And it isn't really another country Mother, since Ireland is part of the United Kingdom."

"Quite," said Charles, "the Irish system is more liberal, treating women doctors and medical students with respect. I can't see Letty being exposed to the hostility and shocking violence that she was subjected to in Edinburgh."

Letty continued, "I am old enough to make this decision without your permission, but I would be grateful to have your blessing and support." She looked at Charles and added, "just like Charles and George did when they went to medical school."

Her father spoke again, "How do you propose funding this course of study?"

"The same way I would have if I'd been allowed to study here, except I will have the added expense of accommodation and meals," she replied, "The legacy from Grandmama will be more than sufficient for the four years of study. Before she died she said to me, "I am leaving you a legacy Letitia dear, use it to pursue your dream." Her eyes were moist as she mentioned the grandmother she was so fond of.

"Hmmph," her father grumbled, "you know my advice is to keep that money invested Letitia," he always used her full name whilst in officious mode.

"Spoken like a true banker Father, but I am now going to

invest the money in my medical education and career," she responded.

Her mother looked appealingly at her father but he just shook his head.

"I can see where your mother stands on this matter, but I cannot give you my blessing and support in this venture, *if,* he emphasised the word, "you are accepted on the course."

Letty looked at him, stung and deeply disappointed, she said, "I am very disappointed in you Father, that you don't have the courage of your convictions." She stuck her chin out defiantly. It was a gesture her mother recognised and her heart sank as to how this would end. "Your so-called support of women being entitled to equal access to education as men, is just words. You supported Charles and George, and yet, when it comes to me, you are treating me as less deserving of the chance to be a doctor. I will be going to Dublin in the Autumn, with or without your blessing, although I would prefer that it was with it." Then she turned to her mother, "Mother, your blessing means so much to me, thank you." and she strode out of the room purposefully.

Her mother said, "I can see, Charles, that you and Letty have been colluding behind our backs, like you so often did in childhood."

"I wholeheartedly support Letty in her ambition and I do feel it is unfair your being so against her Father." But their father stubbornly refused to be moved and relations between him and his daughter had been curt and cool ever since.

Present day

"I DON'T THINK he will be very happy that I have been accepted. I think he was hoping that I wouldn't be offered a place, but I am not going to let that dampen my joy today. This is the best news ever!" she said excitedly, as she buttered toast and poured herself a cup of tea. "I must go and see the others Mother, I expect we all got the same letter, then I must go and tell Louisa, she'll be so happy for me."

"Alright dear, but don't tire Louisa out, she's still weak after her illness."

"I won't tire her Mother, Louisa says my visits give her a boost and brighten her day. Besides, I want to see my gorgeous goddaughter."

"Do be careful on that bicycle Letitia, the traffic around here is getting busier by the week."

"Don't worry Mother, I'll be very careful, I won't let anything come between me and my degree and that includes Father." With that, she hurried upstairs to change into clothes suitable for cycling.

AS EXPECTED, the other five women had been accepted on the course too. However, it was by no means certain that all six would or could take up the place offered.

At yet another coffee morning in Lauder Road (Letty had named it "*The Edinburgh Six* Headquarters") they aired their hopes and fears.

Marion McNair was waiting to hear from a trust fund that gave grants to "gentlewomen in distress", meaning, of course, financial distress or impecunious circumstances.

Emmeline Franks, Juliette Whitton and Victoria Browne were hoping their families would pay the, not inconsiderable, costs. Juliette and Victoria's parents were worried about them going so far from home, and this would determine whether they would provide funds, or not.

Only Letty and Jessica Wilmott were sure of what they needed, in terms of support and finance. Letty felt for the others who who were not in as fortunate a financial position as herself. "Oh dear," she said, "I was hoping so much that all six of us would go and take Dublin by storm."

"We may yet do that Letty," said Emmeline, "I'm not giving up hope."

"Me neither," echoed the others.

"We have to accept or decline the offer by the 31 of August," Letty reminded them, "so use all your womanly powers of persuasion."

They all hoped they would go together in the autumn, but secretly, three thought they would not be so lucky. Only time would tell.

14

FUNDING STRATEGY MEETING
LAUDER ROAD

Letty wasn't a woman for letting the grass grow under her feet, as the saying goes, and so she had a restless night, during which she mulled over the financial difficulties that Marion and Victoria faced. Just before dawn, as a grey light rose in the east, a solution came to her on the cusp of sleep.

Later that morning she cycled around, informing her friends that she was calling a meeting on Saturday morning, the 23rd, to discuss a strategy for funding Marion and Victoria's training costs for the duration of the course.

They were becoming used to these hastily-called meetings at the headquarters of the *Edinburgh Six* and everyone looked forward to the freshly ground coffee and shortbread, still warm from the oven. Since she had organised their tutorials with Dr Cunningham, the group, by tacit agreement, looked to Letty to take the lead.

The usual babble of excited voices accompanied the women into the house, having left their bicycles standing neatly against the side wall.

"Welcome ladies!" said Letty, "help yourselves to coffee and shortbread."

When they were all settled, sitting around the dining-room table, Letty began.

"First of all, I have been thinking about our acceptance letters and I suggest that we write to Dublin immediately, letting them know that we are all accepting their offer of places."

"But what about the money to fund it Letty?" asked Marion, "it's alright for some of you, but what if I can't raise the money to go?"

"Same goes for me," said Victoria, "I had a very serious discussion with my parents on Thursday night when I'd told them we had all been accepted."

"Please ladies, just listen to me before you make any more objections," said Letty.

"Sorry," said Victoria.

"Alright," said Marion, still dubious and rather pessimistic.

"I thought that we might use our connections to the suffrage movement and put on some fundraising events throughout August, while at the same time, looking into the possibilities of scholarships or some other form of sponsorship." She looked around at the others' inscrutable expressions and asked, "Well ladies, what do you think?"

There was utter silence for some moments and then Jessica, who was assured of her funding, said, "I, for one, think it's a jolly good idea! After all, what have we got to lose?"

Marion, ever the pessimist, asked, "But won't that be like asking for charity?"

Emmeline replied, "What do you think the Hope Scholarship is Marion?"

"Yes, but we earned that by coming in the first four in the matriculation examination."

"Yes," Juliette intervened, with some asperity, "and the university robbed us of it in the blink of an eye."

"Hear! Hear!" exclaimed Victoria, "and our sisters and brothers in the suffrage movement really supported us when we went to meet the Dean. I'm sure they will be happy to help us raise funds for such an important cause - they all want the opportunity to consult female doctors." she concluded.

Jessica asked, "How do we go about it Letty?" They all knew that Letty's mother was a founding member of the Edinburgh Women's Suffrage Association and served on the committee.

"I shall put it to mother today, but I am sure we will have their wholehearted support. In the meantime, we need to think of some really innovative and exciting events to attract lots of people, and not just members of the Edinburgh Suffrage Association."

"Yes," said Jessica, "and we can possibly recruit new members at the same time, killing two birds with the one stone, if you'll pardon the cruel expression. It will be to the advantage of everyone," she looked at Marion, "so you see Marion, we will be helping each other, so it's not asking for charity. We shall be earning it by putting on events."

Marion, feeling a little ashamed of her earlier pessimism, brightened and replied, "Yes, I do see what you mean, you've convinced me." she laughed.

"I also think it would be worth contacting the *Scotsman* and *Evening News* and ask them to do an article for us or, if not, we can pay for an advertisement," said Letty.

Juliette said, "We could also get posters printed with the

details of the events and put them up around town, like we do for suffrage recruitment drives and marches."

"Good idea," agreed Letty, "but I have a feeling that the editors of both papers will do a feature, free of charge. After all, they were very supportive over the university debacle and," she looked around the room, "it's bound to boost their circulation if they put it on the front page."

Victoria laughed and said, "I can just see the headlines: "Women robbed of their course places at Edinburgh Medical School and forced to go to Ireland, need funds for their tuition."

"Yes," laughed Juliette, "and I can see Professor Pilkington and his young pups loving us all over again."

Letty said, "Right then ladies, let us adjourn for now and meet again on Monday morning at ten o'clock. In the meantime, I will speak to my mother about getting the Edinburgh Suffrage Association on board. I want you all to bring at least one idea for the fundraising events."

They all left number 8 Lauder Road feeling positive and optimistic about getting sufficient funds so that all six could go to study medicine in Dublin that Autumn.

15

PUTTING "FUN" INTO FUNDRAISING
SATURDAY 23RD - MONDAY 25TH JULY 1887

Letty had not been idle over the weekend. On Saturday her mother promised to call a special meeting of the EWSA committee to discuss hosting a fundraising event which would take place the following month. She had told Letty that she thought they would be only too happy to help.

In the afternoon she visited Louisa and Charles and told them about the previous day's meeting of the *Edinburgh Six*.

"What a marvellous idea Letty," said Louisa, her face lighting up.

"We are meeting again on Monday to discuss ideas and if you can think of anything, I'd be glad to hear about it." She turned to Charles, "Charles, have you managed to find out anything more regarding scholarships or trust funds?"

"I'm afraid it is as you feared," he replied, "for every one I have enquired about so far, only males are eligible to apply, but I shall keep on looking."

Letty looked crestfallen and Louisa patted her hand consolingly. "We shall have to concentrate all our efforts on fundraising then," Letty said in a resigned tone. "Mother is calling a meeting of the suffrage committee to ask them to host whatever events we come up with," she added.

"I'm sure my mother will agree too," said Louisa, "In fact, I'll tell her about it later as they're coming for supper this evening."

"Thank you. I'm not expecting you to get involved Louisa, she still has to rest doesn't she Charles?" Letty added, turning to her brother.

"Yes indeed, but I'm sure we will both be able to attend at least one of your events," Charles replied.

"Goodness!" exclaimed Louisa, "I'm forgetting my manners, would you like some tea Letty?"

"No, thank you Louisa, I'm dashing off to the *Scotsman* office to hand-deliver a letter enquiring about costs of advertising our events." She got up to go and said, "But I do have time to see my goddaughter before I go."

"She's having a nap, but if you're very quiet you can look in on her," replied Louisa.

When Letty went upstairs to the nursery, she found Harvey lying in front of the door, guarding Evangeline. When Letty arrived, he had come down to see who the visitor was and had returned to his post once he was satisfied it was a friend and after allowing Letty to rub his ears for a few seconds. He stood up as Letty approached the door.

"It's alright Harvey, I'm just going to peep into the room," she said, and he moved aside, seeming to understand what was required of him. Letty opened the door a little and she could see the little girl was sound asleep. Closing the door quietly, she patted Harvey on the head and said, "Well done Harvey, you are a good boy." He wagged his tail at this praise and lay down again as Letty went back downstairs.

. . .

LETTY CLIMBED the stairs of the *Scotsman* building in Cockburn Street and left the letter with the clerk at the reception desk, who reassured her that Mr Cooper would receive it that afternoon. She came away satisfied that the wheels had been set in motion to get them all to Dublin.

Monday 25th July

Once more the six women gathered around the dining table in 8 Lauder Road. Letty began, "I've been doing a lot of thinking since Saturday and I have come up with an idea for the form our events might take." They were all looking at her in anticipation. She continued, "What do you think of having a bazaar over a three day period, say Thursday, Friday and Saturday, during the last week in August?"

"That's a brilliant idea Letty," said Victoria, full of enthusiasm, "I was at one just before Christmas and it was fabulous. There were all kinds of stalls selling crafts and other hand made goods, a puppet show for children and even a concert one evening."

"I was at one when I visited relations in London," said Jessica, "and they produced a 'Bazaar Book' as a souvenir which they sold for one shilling." There were appreciative sounds around the table, the idea had really caught their imaginations. "I'll bring the one I bought to our next meeting."

"Wonderful," said Letty.

"Was it just stalls, apart from the puppet show and concert?" asked Marion.

"Oh no, they had competitions too."

"What kind of competitions? Cakes and things?" Juliette asked with interest.

"Yes, there were baking competitions, but also fun ones

like a clothes washing competition for men and a whistling one for women. It was hilarious and so much fun for everyone." They all laughed at the images conjured up by her words.

"Excellent!" exclaimed Letty, "we need to work fast and we must be methodical. First of all we must decide on a date, duration, types of stall, competitions etc, and, most important, a venue."

"I've just had a thought," said Emmeline, "we obviously don't have the time to produce a Bazaar Book, but what about a commemorative programme?"

"Yes, and we could charge for it, less than a shilling, of course, being much smaller than a book."

They continued to discuss the details in organising the bazaar, with everyone putting in their 'tuppence worth'.

"Alright," Letty called the meeting to order again. "Let's set the date and decide on the duration."

The one I went to in London was held over a week," Jessica said, "but that's probably too long for here and I think a one-day event would involve as much work as a five-day event."

Letty was consulting a calendar, "How about three days, Thursday to Saturday, the 25th, 26th and 27th of August?"

"Ideal", "excellent", "wonderful" was heard from around the table.

"That gives us four and a half weeks to prepare," said Letty, "now what about the venue?"

Victoria said, "The Christmas one I went to was in the Waverley Market. It's very spacious, but it smells of the railway station and coal dust."

"What about the Assembly Rooms in George Street?" asked Juliette. "It's spacious and the various rooms can be used for the different aspects of the bazaar, like stalls, competitions etc."

They were all familiar with the layout of the Assembly Rooms, since the suffragists used them for recruitment drives and large meetings.

Those decisions made, they were each given tasks to carry out before the next meeting.

"What about advertising and publicity?" Emmeline asked.

"Good question," replied Letty, "I have written to Mr Cooper, the editor of the *Scotsman,* and I'm hoping to hear back from him before we meet again. Ideally, we want to start advertising and putting up posters by the end of this week."

Marion asked, "When is the next meeting?"

"Shall we meet here at ten o'clock on Friday?" suggested Letty, "does that give everyone sufficient time to do their tasks?"

"I think so!" they chorused.

"Good," said Letty and she showed them out.

16

THE SCOTSMAN TO THE RESCUE

Letty received a reply from the editor by first post on Tuesday. To her surprise, he invited her to meet with him on Wednesday morning at nine-thirty.

Mr Cooper was a large, genial man and he stood up to greet Letty when his clerk showed her into his office. It was quite a small office, Letty noted with surprise. She thought the office of the editor of such a prominent newspaper would have been larger. His desk was large though, and it was littered with rival publications.

"Good morning Miss Frobisher," he said, shaking her hand vigorously, "please, sit down." He indicated a chair by the side of his desk.

"Thank you Mr Cooper," said Letty as she sat down.

"Now, Miss Frobisher, I understand from your letter that you and your five friends are trying to raise funds to enable two of your group, without private means, to take up the places offered to them by the Medical School in Dublin. Is that correct?"

"It is indeed Mr Cooper, and we were wondering about the cost of advertising the event that we are planning."

"I see," he said sounding very interested and enthusiastic. "Tell me about the event."

Letty told him about the three-day Bazaar, planned for the end of August and that the Edinburgh Women's Suffrage Association had agreed to help them to put it on. Her mother had informed her the previous evening that the committee was behind them and their proposed event. They had also been fortunate in booking the Assembly Rooms in George Street.

"This is most enterprising Miss Frobisher, if I may say so."

"Thank you Mr Cooper. We were at a loss as to what to try next since, being women, we were not eligible for any of the scholarships and trust funds we enquired about. They are for males only."

"Tut, tut," he said, sounding annoyed, "I must say that the University of Edinburgh has treated you very badly, with not even a shred of fair play."

"Thank you," Letty replied, "we feel it is very harsh and unjust that the Hope Scholarships, won fairly, have been rescinded, along with our offer of places. This is why we are having to travel to Ireland to do our training. The loss of the scholarships was very hard on two of our members, who shall remain anonymous, for reasons of confidentiality."

"Quite!" the editor agreed.

"So, with regards to having a half-page advertisement, what kind of costs do we need to budget for?" Letty asked.

"The blue eyes regarded her for a few moments and then twinkled as he said, "Miss Frobisher, in the light of your recent shocking experience, at the hands of the university staff and students; your excellent marks in the matriculation examination; and the sympathy and support that poured into my newspaper, I will make you a proposition."

"Yes?" Letty asked a little uncertain at what was about to be said.

"Instead of charging you to advertise your event and the reason for your necessity in doing so, I will do a feature on the *Edinburgh Six* and why such brave and enterprising women should receive the support from the citizens of Edinburgh."

Letty was speechless for some seconds, before finding her voice, "Oh my goodness Mr Cooper, that would be wonderful. Thank you, thank you from the bottom of my heart and on behalf of my five friends."

"Leave it with me Miss Frobisher and I will have a front page headline with part of your story, which will be concluded in the centre with a poster-type announcement for your bazaar," the editor informed her. "I will have a draft delivered to you by tomorrow and once you are happy with it, we will print it in Saturday's edition."

"Again, Mr Cooper, I am so grateful. Would it be possible to invite potential stall holders to make enquiries to me at a Post Office box number?"

"Yes, of course. Do you have a preliminary list of what will be in your bazaar?"

"Yes, I brought a list of possible events, but it's not an exhaustive one I'm afraid." Letty went into her capacious handbag and handed the list to the editor. "I'll go directly to the GPO and arrange a post box for bazaar-related correspondence. I'll give your clerk a note of it on my way back."

"Fine. I'll get on with the article right away Miss Frobisher and you will have a draft copy by tomorrow afternoon at the latest. That will give us Friday to do any amendments before it goes to press.."

"I cannot thank you enough Mr Cooper, from all of us."

"Come back from Ireland as fully-fledged doctors and that will be thanks enough for me."

Letty stood up and shook the editor's outstretched hand. "Good day Mr Cooper."

"Good day to you Miss Frobisher."

Letty was so buoyed up by the outcome of the meeting that she lightly ran up the *Scotsman Steps* from Cockburn Street to the North Bridge and then walked on air to the General Post Office at the corner of North Bridge and Waterloo Place.

HAVING ARRANGED the hire of the post box and left a note of the number with Mr Cooper's clerk, Letty went home for some lunch before setting to work on the programme for the bazaar.

Her mother was at home and they lunched together. "How did your meeting go Letty dear?" Mrs Frobisher smiled fondly at her daughter, "I can see by your flushed appearance that it went well."

"Oh Mother, it was incredible. Mr Cooper has kindly offered to do a feature article on *The Edinburgh Six* and why we need to raise funds. There will be a centre page spread advertising the bazaar and calling for stall-holders and entertainers. That's a huge amount of free advertising, isn't it just wonderful?" She stopped to take a breath as her words and sentences had tumbled out at speed.

Her mother agreed, "That is indeed very generous. It restores one's faith in human nature after the diabolical way the university treated the six of you."

"That was one of the main reasons Mr Cooper wanted to help, that and our examination results, plus the amount of public sympathy that poured into his newspaper. The only upsetting thing that remains is Father's stubborn opposition to me going. Can't you talk to him Mother?"

"Letty dear, I've talked to him until I am blue in the face. Charles has also spoken to him. We will just have to hope that he comes around before you leave."

"I suppose so," she said resignedly, "I abhor this coldness between us."

"Let's leave that subject for now dear. Do you have any plans for this afternoon? Do you want to come shopping with me?"

"Thank you for the offer Mother, but I want to make a start on the programme, time is of the essence, as they say. I want to have the final draft ready for our meeting on Friday, so any changes can be agreed on before it goes to the printers. We want to start putting the posters up as soon as possible."

"Alright darling, I'll see you at supper," she said, but she could see that her daughter's mind was already on the programme for the bazaar. She smiled and went to get ready for her afternoon's outing.

17

SATURDAY, 30TH JULY 1887

Every one of the *Edinburgh Six* were up early on Saturday morning, eager to buy the *Scotsman* and to read the article and the large advertisement for the bazaar.

Letty had told them on Friday about her meeting with Mr Cooper and the wonderful news that he was producing a feature on the plight of two of them as well as the free advertising. He had also said that the Evening news would carry it too, to ensure as wide a coverage as possible.

THE FRONT PAGE article read as follows:

"The Women Who Have No Choice But to Go To Ireland To Become Doctors

IN APRIL OF THIS YEAR, six Edinburgh women passed the matriculation examination for admission onto the medical degree course at Edinburgh University. They took the top six places, ahead of all the other entrants, who were male.

The Hope Scholarship is awarded each year to the four top-scoring entrants in the matriculation examination. However, a short time later, the university rescinded the scholarships and the offer of places on the course.

Readers may remember the public outrage at the shocking treatment those women suffered at the hands of the university court and the violence perpetrated on them, by a mob of medical students, as they arrived to meet with the Dean of the Medical Faculty. They were pelted with missiles and one lady had to have stitches in a head wound after being struck with a stone.

Now the women must leave their homes and families and travel to Ireland in order to gain their medical degrees. Sadly, two of them will not be able to take up their places in Dublin if the money for their fees and living expenses cannot be raised. Both women had been relying on the Hope Scholarship awarded to them, to pay for them to study.

The women, supported by the Edinburgh Women's Suffrage Association, are holding a special three-day event towards the end of August, to try to raise the much needed funds. Details of this event can be found in the centre pages of today's paper.

Everyone here at the *Scotsman* wishes them success and we hope that the noble people of Edinburgh will get behind them and support this effort. We would like all six to go and study in Dublin, as they would have done here, if the university had not robbed them of their funding and places.

Good luck ladies!

. . .

THE ADVERTISEMENT WAS AS FOLLOWS:

"GRAND BAZAAR
In aid of female doctors
Will be held in
The Assembly Rooms, George Street
from Thursday 25th to Saturday 27th August
9am - 6pm
Admission 4d. (children free)

Capacity for 75 stalls for arts, crafts and home-made goods
10/- per day or £1.5/- for 3 days
Apply to: Miss Frobisher PO Box No. 157

* COMPETITIONS *
Gentlemen's clothes washing competition
Ladies whistling competition
Ladies nail hammering competition
Bakery competition: cakes, shortbread etc
Flower arranging
Embroidery
Entry 3d.

* ENTERTAINMENT *
Puppet Show
Conjuring
Ladies String Quartet
Admission 3d

* DEMONSTRATIONS *
Scottish Country Dancing
Highland Dancing
Weaving
Lace-making
Admission 3d.

*FORTUNE-TELLING *
By Gypsy Rose Lee - 6d.
Commemorative Programme - 1/-

* GRAND BALL *
Saturday 27th August - 8pm
Tickets £2 - includes refreshments
Music by Walter Smythe Orchestra
Donations for prizes gratefully accepted

THE SIX FRIENDS met at Lauder Road for afternoon tea and to discuss the newspaper article and advertisement.

"I'll say this for Mr Cooper," said Jessica, "he certainly let the university know what he thinks of them."

"He did indeed, but what a good article," said Marion, "I hope lots of people read about us and come to the bazaar."

Letty said, "We still have a lot of work to do over the coming weeks," she looked at Emmeline and asked, "how did you get on at the printers?"

"Very well," Emmeline replied, "the posters and handbills will be ready for collection on Monday."

They discussed what needed to be done and tasks were allocated to ensure maximum publicity for the event, delegating jobs, where possible, to their friends in the suffrage union as well as involving their families to help out.

As they got up and gathered their things to leave, Letty said, "One last thing, have you all written to Dublin accepting your offer of a place?"

"Yes, of course!" they chorused.

"Good!" said Letty.

18

AN UNEXPECTED OUTCOME

The Dean of the Medical Faculty, Professor Smithson, read the *Scotsman* article with interest. He had heard about them all being offered places, at the King and Queen's College in Dublin, from Letty, but he hadn't been aware that there was any financial impediment to taking up the offer.

He thought, yet again, about the way the women had been treated by the university, especially the Faculty of Medicine. The fact that two of them might not be able to become doctors, due to a lack of funds, made him feel both ashamed and angry. The more so when he thought about the Hope Scholarships going the very same young men who had committed such violence against them.

He was pacing his office as he thought. It was often his practice to go into work on a Saturday, as there was no one at home. His wife had died many years ago, giving birth to the child who also died just a few hours after she was born. He looked out the window onto Middle Meadow Walk and wondered, if life hadn't been so cruel, would his daughter have followed his footsteps into medicine? "Not much chance of her doing that in this damned university," he said angrily to the empty room. He guessed that Miss Letitia Frobisher was around the age that Constance would have been, had she survived. They had chosen names early on in Eliza's pregnancy, Constance Eliza if the baby was a girl and Henry William if it was a boy.

He pulled himself back from such painful memories and into the present day. "Work," he thought "has thankfully been my salvation. I wonder..." he said again to the room, and then he sat down at his desk, took a sheet of paper from the drawer and started to write a letter.

Professor Pilkington also saw the article while he was having breakfast at home, in Abercromby Place, in the New Town. He was about to swallow a piece of toast when he read the editor's censuring of the university. As he threw down the paper in disgust, he choked on the toast as it went down the wrong way. His eyes watered as he coughed in an effort to clear his windpipe and, as he was mopping his face, he was already composing in his mind, a suitably, strongly-worded letter to the *Scotsman*.

He went to his study, having abandoned the remains of his meal, and sat down at his desk. He took a sheet of paper and began to write the letter. Every now and then, he stopped as he fumed at the audacity of the man. "How dare he? How *dare* he?" He was almost apoplectic as he penned his rebuke of the *Scotsman* in general and the editor, Mr Cooper, in particular. "Blast their obscene liberalism!" he shouted.

His wife, Muriel, knocked on the door and entered the study. "Are you alright dear? What is all the commotion about?"

"It's those blasted women again and the *Scotsman*," he blustered.

"But I thought the university had banned them from the course," she said, rather confused.

"We have," he retorted, "but the damned editor of that paper is trying to raise funds so they can go to Ireland to get their degrees."

"Oh, I see," was all that Muriel could come up with. Secretly, she was in favour of women doctors, but for the sake of peace, she kept this opinion to herself.

"But why would the *Scotsman's* helping them make you so angry dear?" she ventured, "surely that's all in the past, months ago, over and done with?"

He literally yelled at his wife, "Not when the editor is criticising the university and the students for the way they were treated."

"I'll leave you to your letter dear," said Mrs Pilkington in a calm voice and she withdrew quietly from the room.

By the middle of the week following the publication of the article, the *Edinburgh Evening News* had also covered the story of *The Edinburgh Six*.

Mail bags full of letters from the public and readership of both newspapers, were arriving daily with not only words of support, but some with pledges of money towards the fees for the two women who had been dependent on the Hope Scholarship.

In the light of such generosity, Mr Cooper announced the *Scotsman Appeal Fund,* detailing how donations could be made and that "no amount is too small since every penny counts".

Letty and her friends were astounded as the public

support grew and played out before their eyes, with each new edition of the newspapers.

On Saturday the 6th August, Letty received a letter from Mr Cooper, inviting her to a meeting with him at ten o'clock on Monday morning.

On Monday morning, puzzled and a little apprehensive, she left the house in Lauder Road to keep her appointment with the editor.

When the clerk showed her into Mr Cooper's office, she could see, at a glance, that something had happened. He could barely contain his excitement. "Ah, good morning Miss Frobisher," he greeted her and shook her hand. "Please do sit down, I have some good news for you."

Any apprehension Letty had entered the room with, melted away with the editor's demeanour.

"I must say that the public's response to your need to raise funds is overwhelming. Donations are pouring in and, so far, they amount to £275," he smiled broadly at her her.

"This is wonderful news Mr Cooper, it bodes well for our bazaar at the end of the month." She returned his beaming smile.

"Ah, but that is not all Miss Frobisher," he said. "I received a letter at the end of last week, from a gentleman who has offered to meet any deficit between what is raised from your bazaar and public donations and the amount required for fees and a living allowance for both women. The only condition placed on this offer is that the donor shall remain anonymous."

He sat back in his chair and placed his hands over his ample stomach, smiling from ear to ear. "Well, what do you think Miss Frobisher? It looks like your two friends will be going to Dublin with you after all."

Letty, for once, was speechless. "Well ... I ..." She shook

her head and then, finding speech, she replied, "Well, it sounds wonderful Mr Cooper. Is it a genuine offer, do you think? Not a medical student playing a prank?"

"I can assure you that it is a genuine offer from an authentic and well-respected person."

"Oh my goodness!" she exclaimed, her hand going to her mouth as thoughts tumbled across her mind. "I can't wait to tell Marion and Victoria, she said, gathering up her things.

She stopped abruptly, realising she had inadvertently given the names of the two women who were supposed to remain confidential. She looked stricken, but Mr Cooper said, "Don't worry about that slip of the tongue Miss Frobisher, their names will be kept as secret as your generous benefactor's."

"Thank you, my excitement made me careless. However, we still have to try and raise as much as we can so that our secret donor knows we are not taking his generous offer for granted."

She shook his hand, saying, "Would you please thank this wonderful person on behalf of *The Edinburgh Six*?"

"With pleasure Miss Frobisher. Good day to you."

"Good day Mr Cooper," said Letty and she hurried to let the others know about the marvellous offer from an unknown person.

19

THE JOURNEY BEGINS
WEDNESDAY 28TH SEPTEMBER 1887

On a crisp, clear, early Autumn morning, *The Edinburgh Six* waited on Platform 1 of the Waverley Station, ready to board the train that would take them on to the next chapter of their lives. The women were accompanied by families and friends who had gathered to give them a rousing send-off, as they embarked on the first stage of their medical education and, indeed, careers. That is to say, the others were accompanied by their families, but Letty's father had not relented and she was leaving Edinburgh without his support and blessing. Despite the excitement of the occasion, Letty felt a deep sadness that her father was not marking one of the most important days of her life. Her mother, Charles and Louisa were there and they too felt her sadness caused by her father's absence.

The Edinburgh Women's Suffrage Association, who had been instrumental in putting on the Bazaar and generally helping with fundraising, had sent a contingent to wave them off, complete with a brass band.

The railway guards and drivers looked on in wonder,

they hadn't seen anything like it since a touring opera company had arrived at their station.

There were also reporters, not only from the *Scotsman, Evening News* and *Glasgow Herald*, but from some of the nationals, including a correspondent for the *Manchester Guardian*, who had been following the story of *The Edinburgh Six* from a distance. Their rejection by Edinburgh University and subsequent struggle to find a medical school who would accept them, had received much publicity throughout the country, as well as support for their cause. Even the *Irish Times* had a notice on the front page telling its readers about the "Scottish colleens" who had to come to Ireland to get their medical degrees.

THE BAZAAR "in aid of female doctors" had been a huge success and saw hundreds of people visiting on each day of the three-day event. Everyone involved worked extremely hard to make it a success. Entertainers had waived their fees and performed free of charge, which meant all of the admission money went straight to the cause.

Several members of the suffrage movement had dressed up as famous women from history, including Helen of Troy, Joan of Arc, Queen Bodicea, Queen Elizabeth, her cousin, Mary Queen of Scots and many more. Their role was to act as ushers: some out in the street to attract people in; others acting as stewards, directing people to the various stalls and events. As an unexpected outcome, there was great interest in the suffrage movement and many women joined the Edinburgh Women's Suffrage Association.

Some of the competitions were very popular and attracted large numbers paying 3d. each to watch men attempting to wash clothes, with its unintentional but hilarious slapstick outcomes.

The women's whistling competition was equally popular and Louisa was a surprising runner-up to the winner's very tuneful rendition of "Greensleeves".

Letty and her friends entered the nail-hammering competition with great enthusiasm and finesse and were placed in the top three. The judge remarked that, "It is a good omen for the intricate operations they are sure to perform in their chosen careers" and everyone laughed at the image this produced in their minds.

The Bazaar Ball, marking the end of the three days of raising funds, was also a huge success in its own right. It was a fabulous, glittering affair. The three ballroom chandeliers, lit by a total of three hundred candles, combined with the many wall lights, created a sparkling rainbow effect, when reflected on the women's jewellery, as couples glided around on the dance floor.

All in all, donations from the public to the *Scotsman's* appeal, some as generous as thirty pounds or more each, plus the proceeds of the Bazaar and Ball, raised just over three quarters of the amount required. With the remainder of the money promised by their secret benefactor, Marion McNair and Victoria Browne were assured of their places at the King and Queen's College of Physicians, along with the other four women.

AND NOW THE time that they had all dreamed of had finally come and they were about to depart. It would be a long and tiring voyage, involving two train journeys and an overnight sailing on the ferry from Liverpool to Kingstown, which served Dublin as a port.

As they waited by their first class carriage, their trunks having already been stowed in the guards van, Edinburgh suffragist, Margaret MacDonald, played the first few bars of the old Scots favourite, "Auld Lang Syne". Everyone there sang the words as tears welled up in the eyes of those leaving home, aa well as the family members who were seeing them off. Letty felt a hand on her shoulder and she turned around to see her father standing beside her, with tears not far from the surface of his eyes. He embraced her and said, "My darling Letty, I am so proud of you and I give you my blessing. Do well my dear." She hugged him tightly as the others looked on, touched and so relieved by him turning up at last.

There was a great cheer and shouts of "Good luck to you all!" at the end of the song, along with much hugging and kissing as the guard blew his whistle announcing the train's imminent departure. Letty and the others leaned out of the carriage windows as the banging of carriage doors was heard the length of the train.

As the train began to move slowly away, mothers, fathers, sisters and brothers walked alongside calling out endearments. They carried on to the end of the platform and stood waving as the train picked up speed and disappeared around a bend, leaving only smoke and steam behind.

The Frobishers dried their eyes and made their sombre way up the Waverley steps and walked along Princes Street to Jenners for morning coffee in the Garden Room restaurant.

"Come on everyone," Louisa said, once they'd given their order to the waitress and, trying to lighten the mood, added coaxingly, "this is a happy occasion, they are now following their dreams."

Charlotte Frobisher dabbed her eyes with a lace handkerchief and said, "I know Louisa, it's just that I shall miss her so. The house will be so quiet." She gave her daughter-in-law a weak smile, "I'd even got used to her having *The Edinburgh Six* commandeering my dining room on a regular basis."

Louisa returned her smile and replied, "They'll be *The Dublin Six* now and, in four years time, when they come back to us as fully qualified doctors, women in Edinburgh will have a choice of whether to consult a man or a woman."

"Yes, you're right Louisa dear, and she'll be home for Christmas, that'll be something to look forward to."

With their spirits lighter, they had their coffee and talked of other things.

ON THE TRAIN they all talked excitedly about the term that was about to begin the following Monday.

"I'm glad the first week is for orientation," said Victoria, "it will give us time to settle into our accommodation and to become a bit more familiar with Dublin."

They were all going to be staying in a hostel for women students which had a house warden to make sure the women were safe and well and that the rules were strictly adhered to.

"I just can't wait for the lectures to start on Monday week," said Letty, "we've waited so long and worked so hard for that day to dawn."

"Hear! Hear!" chorused the others.

Marion, the perpetual worrier in the group, said, "I do hope the crossing tonight isn't too rough. I've never been on a boat before, so I hope I won't be seasick."

To her consternation, the others looked at her and burst out laughing.

"Oh Marion," said Emmeline, "don't worry, if you are sick we shall start our clinical work early and look after you."

Their change of trains in York for Liverpool went smoothly and *The Edinburgh Six* disembarked in Kingstown at seven-thirty the next morning, none the worse for the crossing.

20

LETTERS FROM LETTY
SEPTEMBER TO OCTOBER 1887

30th September 1887 - a picture postcard

DEAREST LOUISA AND CHARLES,

We arrived safe and well in Kingstown early yesterday morning after a, mercifully, calm crossing. I have heard that the Irish Sea can be very rough so we counted our blessings. We are settling in at the student house and getting to see a bit of Dublin before our orientation week commences on Monday. I hope you like this postcard of O'Connell Bridge which spans the Liffey.

Sending you both all my love and special kisses to my beautiful goddaughter, Evangeline.

Letty xx

ST JAMES STUDENT HOUSE,
    St James Street,
    Kilmainham,
    Dublin

5th October 1887

Dearest Louisa and Charles,

I trust this letter finds you well, as am I. I am writing this from a desk in the student house library. The desk is by a large window which looks out over the gardens adjoining the nearby St James's Catholic Church. The house is very comfortable and we are fortunate that the friendly warden arranged for us all to be accommodated in the one six-bed dormitory. Everyone is very welcoming and apparently our "reputation" had gone before us, courtesy of an article in the Irish Times! What do you think of your sister being (in)famous Charles?

The medical school is attached to St Steeven's Hospital, a bit like the Edinburgh Medical School and the Royal Infirmary I suppose, and it's situated south of the Quays, not far from the River Liffey.

Lectures are very interesting and we can't thank Dr Cunningham enough for giving us such a good grounding in the subjects we are studying now, in more depth. If you see him, please tell him that we all send him our warmest regards.

It will be a little while before we will be "let loose" on the wards, but when the time comes, it will be interesting since our lecturers will also be our clinical teachers there. I really do think they have a most excellent way of doing things in the Dublin Medical School.

We are all becoming more familiar with the area around the hospital and student house and in our spare time, when not studying, we are enjoying exploring the shops and tea and coffee houses.

Please give my love to Ma and Pa Charles, tell them I will write soonest and that they don't have to worry about me since our house warden does that. There are very strict rules around times and we must be back in by nine o'clock, when the door is locked, unless we have a special pass for going to the theatre etc.

I shall sign off now, as I don't have any more news at this time and the others are waiting for me as we are going into town for luncheon.

ALL MY LOVE ALWAYS,
    Letty xx

ST JAMES STUDENT HOUSE,
    St James Street,
    Kilmainham,
    Dublin.
    Saturday 29th October 1887

DEAREST CHARLES AND LOUISA,

Thank you for your letter with all the news from Edinburgh. I must say that it surprised me that I found myself feeling very homesick, as your words brought to mind images of people and places.

The leaves on the trees are certainly on the turn here, as Autumn takes a firm hold and I can imagine how beautiful the Meadows must be now, with the array of gold and copper-coloured leaves drifting down and carpeting the footpaths and grass.

However, I am taking a good grip of myself as I remind myself that I chose to train to become a doctor and, since I was deprived of doing so in Edinburgh, I shall enjoy the sights and scents of Autumn in St Stephen's Green and around Dublin.

How exciting to hear that you are getting your own carriage

soon and how fortunate that you have a mews for stabling and accommodation for your driver. Yes, I think Mr Brown's son will be very reliable following in his father's footsteps, who has been with Lord and Lady Moncrieff for many years.

It's so lovely to hear that Evangeline and Harvey adore each other so. He is such a sweet, gentle soul and my goddaughter is such a darling girl. I can't wait to see her, and you all of course, at Christmas, but before that time comes, I have to work hard and do well in the end of term examinations.

It's not all hard work though, as we are exploring nearby towns. We went to Dundalk last Saturday which is about halfway between Dublin and Belfast. We took the train and enjoyed lovely coastal views. It's a big town with lots of ancient history attached.

There is much discussion and debate here around the issue of "home rule" and the splits in Parliamentary parties etc. To be honest, it sounds very complex and I don't pretend to understand it. However, it is important to many who want to be independent from the United Kingdom.

We are all members of the Dublin Women's Suffrage Association which is very active and is a broad church comprising nationalists and unionists, Protestants and Catholics. Discussions can become very heated before the chairwoman restores order by reminding everyone that the women's franchise is the priority over all else. It's most entertaining Louisa, I wish you could be there at times.

Well my darlings, I have just looked at the clock and I must meet the others in five minutes for an outing. Today, we're lunching at Sandypoint Beach.

WITH ALL MY LOVE,
Letty x

21

DECEMBER 1887

Letty and her friends passed their end of term examinations with the high marks that were becoming the hallmark of these bright young women. Their tutors were well-pleased with the popular Scottish contingent, known to all at the medical school as *The Edinburgh Six*. They were looking forward to going home for Christmas, after all their hard work over the recent months.

The crossing from Kingstown to Liverpool was a rough one with the choppy waters of the Irish Sea being whipped up by gale force winds.

The ferry was due to dock in Liverpool at three o'clock on the 21st of December and they were glad that they had decided to spend the night in Liverpool ahead of their onward train journeys to Edinburgh. They felt very bedraggled and bone-weary from being tossed about in their cabins.

They gathered their valises and walked shakily down the gangplank, holding fast to the rail, for the ferry was still moving on the swell, even in the harbour.

Victoria, who was the one most affected by seasickness,

tried to quell the lingering nausea and said, "I am so glad you suggested spending the night here Letty, I don't think I could travel another mile today."

"I couldn't agree more," said Marion, pulling her hat firmly onto her head in the brisk breeze blowing in from the sea.

"Ladies, let's join the queue for a hackney cab, the sooner we check in at the hotel, the better." said Letty.

"Lead on MacDuff," quipped Jessica, who was brightening up by the minute as she found her "land legs" again. Although it was just after three o'clock, it was almost dark and sleet was beginning to blow down from the north.

Their arrival at the Adelphi Hotel, in the centre of Liverpool, was met with a flurry of activity from porters and the receptionist. The formalities completed, the women were taken to their first floor accommodation where fires had been lit against the December chill. They occupied a suite of rooms comprising a sitting room and three double bedrooms.

After showing them where the bathrooms were, the porter asked, "Would you ladies like to have afternoon tea brought up or would you care to come to the dining room?"

They looked at each other, their slightly battered appearance was a tell-tale sign of their travel-weariness. Then they all looked at Letty and she replied, "Oh here if you please. We shall all want a hot bath before dinner."

"As you wish madam," the porter said bowing, "I shall have it brought up to your sitting room straight away."

"Thank you so much," she peered at his name badge and, taking a shilling from her reticule, she handed it to him saying, "thank you George."

"Very generous madam," he said turning the extremely generous tip over in his hand.

They all ate heartily of the dainty sandwiches, scones and little cakes and, even Victoria whose nausea had abated enjoyed the little feast.

"Well that certainly hit the spot," said Juliette, sitting back and dabbing her mouth with a linen napkin. "Who wants to bathe first? There are two bathrooms so it shouldn't take us too long."

Two hours later, rested and feeling much better after their scented baths, the women gathered in the sitting room to go down to dinner.

As they came down the wide, sweeping staircase, Jessica exclaimed, "Look at the beautiful Christmas tree and the pretty decorations!"

They had been so exhausted when they arrived that they had not noticed the large, richly decorated reception hall. There was a spruce tree which must have been at least twenty feet tall, festooned with garlands, colourful glass and china baubles, pine cones and, best of all, lit candles.

"Ooh!" said Emmeline, "there must be at least a hundred candles on the tree."

"Yes, it's quite magical," agreed Letty, "I think we've had our heads in our books so much, that we barely noticed the Christmas decorations in Dublin."

The proprietors of the Adelphi Hotel were very aware of the hazard of having lighted candles on a Christmas tree and had wisely cordoned off a four foot berth around the tree. It was all too easy for clothing to catch fire if someone came too close, or if a lit candle fell from an upper branch, as had happened elsewhere in the city the previous year.

The women sat in the lounge and were served dry sherry whilst their choice of meals was being prepared. They marvelled at how far they had come since April that year, when they had sat the matriculation examination.

"Oh my," said Victoria, "so much has happened since then, I feel like it was another era altogether."

"Yes," said Marion, "I feel like a different person since I've been in Dublin," she shook her head in disbelief and added, "how strange."

Letty said, "Marion, you are a different woman. You are not the timid mouse who travelled to Dublin in September." The others concurred and Letty continued, "You have so much more belief in yourself, you are more confident altogether."

Marion reddened at this uncomfortably accurate summary of herself, but was pleased by the comments and compliments from the others.

Back in the lounge, sipping coffee after dinner, they looked forward with excitement to returning to Edinburgh the next day.

Emmeline asked, "How much do you think Evangeline will have grown Letty? You haven't seen her for the past three months, that's almost a third of her life!"

The other women were always keen to hear about Letty's goddaughter and she was always happy to tell them the latest news after each letter from Louisa arrived.

"I can hardly wait to have her in my arms and kiss her sweet-smelling baby cheek. Of course, she has several teeth now and is almost walking."

They all fell silent, thinking about what each was looking forward to most about going home.

Presently, Juliette yawned and said, "I'm sorry ladies, but I'm so tired and if I don't go to bed now, you will have to carry me upstairs."

Letty said, "Me too, we have an early start tomorrow and *The Edinburgh Six* must look their best when we get off the train at the Waverley." They all trooped off, exhausted but happy, up the stairs to their bedrooms.

Thursday 22nd December 1887

THE TRAIN PUFFED its way into the Waverley Station at precisely five o'clock. It was a wintry evening and sleet was being blown in swirls along Platform 1 by a chilly east wind.

The women collected their cases and bags from the overhead racks and waited, with palpable excitement, for the train to come to a complete stop. A porter was waiting, ready to open the door of their first class compartment and they stepped down onto the platform to a rapturous welcome.

Every one of them had family members, wrapped warmly in coats and furs, waiting to welcome them home. Letty was delighted to see her parents there and they rushed to greet her and hugged her close.

"It's wonderful to see you darling," her mother said, holding her at arms length to look at her. "You do look well, I must say," she continued with a note of surprise in her voice.

Letty laughed and said, "Of course I'm well Mother, we are very well looked after in the student house." The others were having similar conversations with their parents and siblings.

"Let's get you home my dear," said her father, "Louisa and Charles are coming to supper this evening," he said, picking up her luggage, "so you can give us all your news then."

"I am looking forward to seeing Charles, and Louisa of

course, I think we'll have even more than usual to talk about now, even after just one term at medical school."

They all moved off towards the ticket barrier at the same time and the six friends hugged each other saying "Goodbye" and "Happy Christmas". All were in good spirits and even the sooty smell of the Waverley station was welcome.

22

CHRISTMAS DAY 1887

Lord and Lady Moncrieff had invited Louisa and Charles, Charles's parents Henry and Charlotte, and Letty to spend Christmas Day with them at home in Heriot Row. This way, both sets of grandparents would be able to be with Evangeline, on her first Christmas. George, the Frobisher's younger son, was working abroad.

Louisa and her mother loved Christmas and had decorated the tree in the drawing room with colourful garlands and glass and china baubles. The candles would be lit just before the presents were given out after the Christmas meal.

Louisa and Charles arrived at noon and were welcomed by Margaret, Lady Moncrieff's maid.

"Happy Christmas Dr and Lady Louisa. Let me take your coats and hats." She looked at Evangeline who was nine months old today, and she said, "And a Happy First Christmas to you Miss Evangeline."

The little girl was wearing a beautiful red velvet coat trimmed with white fur, which Louisa removed and handed to the maid to put in the cloakroom with theirs.

"What a beautiful girl you are," said Margaret, admiring

the pink dress, also made of velvet and little black pumps of the softest leather.

"Thank you Margaret and a Happy Christmas to you too," said Louisa. "Are my parents in the drawing room?"

"Yes Lady Louisa," said Margaret, who always referred to Louisa using her maiden title, "they're waiting for you. Dr Frobisher's parents and Miss Letty are with them, they arrived a little while ago."

The small family entered the drawing room to greetings of "Happy Christmas" and much hugging.

Lady Moncrieff kissed Louisa's cheek and exclaimed, "Oh my Louisa, you're freezing! Come and sit by the fire and get warmed."

"Thank you Mother," she said, taking the seat her father-in-law had just vacated for her. "It's bitterly cold out, even with the rugs covering us, the cold still managed to penetrate."

Her mother looked at her closely and said, "I think you may not be fully recovered from your illness six months ago."

"Oh Mother, please, let's not talk about that, I am well I promise you, ask Charles," she replied.

But before she could pursue that line of conversation, her father handed out glasses of sherry to everyone. He stood in the centre of the group gathered around the fireplace, raised his glass and said, "Happy Christmas!" The others all raised their glasses and echoed, "Happy Christmas!"

The drawing room was warm and extremely comfortable, with a blazing fire burning in the large marble fireplace. The chandelier in the centre of the ceiling was lit by candles in honour of the occasion and the firelight was reflected and refracted, making the crystal sparkle, as though there were a thousand little lights as well as the candles. The gilt-edged ceiling rose glowed warmly in the suffused light from the gas mantles around the walls.

Letty asked, "May I take Evangeline on my knee please?"

"Of course Aunt Letty can have Evangeline on her knee," said Charles. He and Louisa exchanged excited glances and Charles, who had been carrying his daughter, set her on her feet on the floor. Everyone gasped in delighted surprise as Charles and Louisa, taking a hand each, led a walking and smiling Evangeline towards Letty in faltering, little steps.

Both grandmothers exclaimed at the same time, "She's walking! How wonderful!"

Louisa said, "She is walking with our help, but it won't be long before she is doing so entirely on her own." Both Louisa and Charles were inordinately proud of their clever little daughter.

"Yes," laughed Charles, "Harvey will have to keep his ears out of her reach."

"Where is our brave boy?" asked Lord Moncrieff, who was very fond of the ageing dog and had missed him since he had gone to live with Louisa and Charles eighteen months earlier.

"We thought the journey and the excitement would be too much for him," replied Louisa, "so we've left him at home where he is, no doubt, being spoiled by Mrs Hammond and Gertie who are probably sharing their Christmas dinner with him."

Just then, Margaret entered the room, curtsied and said, "Luncheon is served Lady Moncrieff."

"Thank you Margaret, we will be through directly."

The dining room overlooked the private gardens opposite, where a thick hoar frost clung to the bare branches of the trees and covered the grass in a carpet of white. By contrast, the room was cosy with a large fire in the ornate Georgian fireplace.

The mirror above the fireplace reflected the candlelight from the chandelier, which was even bigger than the one in the drawing room, as well as the soft light from the gas wall lamps.

The mahogany dining table almost groaned under the weight of the festive feast. There were large silver platters of turkey, goose and pheasant; roasted vegetables; Brussel Sprouts and a rich, thick gravy. The crystal glassware sparkled and the silver cutlery gleamed in the light from the lamps and firelight. There was a festive centrepiece that Lady Moncrieff and Louisa had made with pine cones, mistletoe and holly, bearing blood-red berries, arranged around a large red candle.

At each place setting, alongside the napkins, were Christmas crackers, decorated with gold ribbons. These would be pulled later amidst much laughter and anticipation of the little surprises inside.

A "high chair" was set at one end of the table for Evangeline, next to her mother and father, who would help her to eat her little portion of Christmas dinner.

Margaret and Wilma, who came to help when Lord and Lady Moncrieff were entertaining, were serving, along with Mortimer, their footman. They were well trained in the role of remaining unobtrusive whilst serving food and wine. The staff would have the day after Christmas, Boxing Day, for their meal, when they would be presented with their gifts from the family. Only the upper classes in Scotland took time off to celebrate Christmas, the others preferred to make the in-coming New Year a time for celebration on "Hogmanay".

Back in the drawing room, Charles was given the honour

of lighting the candles on the tree and then the lovely colourfully-wrapped presents would be handed round.

They all sat at a safe distance while Charles carefully lifted the lighted spill to each candle, which for safety, was firmly attached to the outermost branches.

Evangeline, who was sitting on Grandfather Moncrieff's knee, clapped her chubby little hands in delight. Louisa looked at her daughter, in the bosom of her family, and could not help but think of her "other children" in the Refuge and Homes, and a pang of pity struck her heart. But, she told herself, that they were very lucky to have been rescued and they had been given little gifts from well-wishers and supporters.

At that moment Charles came over and put his arm around her shoulder and drew her close. He smiled and she knew that Charles had seen the moment of sadness that had briefly crossed her face moments before.

Emily Moncrieff had begun to hand out the presents and she had presented the first one to Evangeline. Sitting on his knee, her grandfather looked at the gift tag and said, "This is for you Evangeline, from Aunt Letty." The little girl laughed and held out her hands. "Shall we open it?" he asked and then he helped her tear the paper and inside was a white velveteen rabbit with a blue ribbon around his neck. She babbled in her own language as she bounced it on his knee.

When everyone had given and received their gifts and had thanked each other whilst enthusing over the others' thoughtfulness and generosity, Lord Moncrieff stood up and carried Evangeline to where a single, large, strangely shaped present was standing, almost out of sight.

His wife, Emily who was in on the surprise, joined them there.

"I wonder what this could be," she said to her granddaughter. Evangeline just smiled and clapped her hands again.

"I think you'd best bring it over here so you can open it and see," said James Moncrieff.

By this time, everyone's interest was aroused and they gathered round to see what it was, as Emily tore off the sheets of wrapping to reveal a rocking horse. It was most beautifully carved in a pale wood with a soft leather saddle and reins with little silver bells. It had a mane of dark hair and was altogether lovely.

"Would you like to sit on the horse Evangeline?" asked her grandfather and he gently sat her on the saddle whilst keeping hold of her.

"She's a little young for it at the moment Father," said Louisa, as her father gently rocked Evangeline back and forth, "but she'll grow into it before too long I'm sure."

"It's such a lovely piece of carpentry," added Charles "thank you on behalf of our daughter."

Evangeline was beginning to nod and Louisa lifted her up. "I think it's time for a nap my darling, let's go up to the nursery and tuck you in."

"I'll come with you." said Letty.

The nursery, which had been Louisa's, had been redecorated in pastel shades, her old cot had been assembled and her soft toys had been arranged around the room.

Louisa changed her napkin and put a little nightgown on her and laid her in the cot. There was a fire in a small grate, covered by a guard, for safety, so the room was warm.

Letty had brought the little white rabbit up with her and laid it beside her niece. Evangeline's thumb found her mouth and she was soon sleeping soundly. Letty stroked her hair and then they both left the room quietly.

Downstairs, coffee and brandy were being served, but Letty and Louisa opted for coffee only, as the brandy would have them asleep in minutes after their elaborate and sumptuous lunch and they had been up early to attend the Christmas carol service at St Giles Cathedral.

James, Henry and Charles were discussing politics, while Emily and Charlotte were talking about the Edinburgh suffrage events for 1888.

"We have been campaigning for twenty years," Charlotte complained, "I wonder what we need to do to get the government to pay attention to us."

"As a matter of fact, Charlotte, it's more disheartening than that, it's more like sixty years," replied Emily, "I remember Mother talking about it. A petition was submitted asking for women's suffrage in the 1832 Reform Bill, which extended it to more men, but no women." She sat reflecting, as though she was looking back down the years. "It was John Stuart Mill who presented the mass petition to parliament in 1866. Sadly, we have been left out of another two Reform Bills since."

"It's not sad Mother," said Louisa, "it's absolutely infuriating."

"Perhaps our demonstrations should become more visible and more demanding," said Letty, "you know, gather outside Downing Street and demand to speak to the Prime Minister. Maybe if we could talk to him, face to face, we might be more persuasive than just thousands of names on a petition. What do you think Louisa?"

"I think it's an excellent idea, or we could do the same outside the House of Commons. I think that would be admirable - in theory," replied Louisa.

"Why only in theory?" asked Letty, feeling slightly let down.

"Well, think about it Letty, women in society are, on the whole, brought up to be part of the background. We don't put ourselves forward or make our voices heard, so it would be a difficult thing for a lot of women to do. It would take a very brave woman to go to Downing Street and actually demand to speak to the Prime Minister."

"Yes," agreed Letty, "I do see what you mean. It feels a bit daring to even walk in a "Votes for Women" procession with people watching us, or shouting at us."

Thus both the men and women spent the next hour or so, putting the world to rights, as it were, until it was time for the visitors to go home.

Lord and Lady Moncrieff kissed their guests goodbye on the steps of 39 Heriot Row, as their carriages arrived to take them home.

"Don't stand in the cold, Mother-in-law," said Charles, "it's bitterly cold. Goodbye and thank you for a wonderful Christmas Day."

The Broughams drove off to a chorus of "goodbyes" and James and Emily returned to the warmth of their drawing room, satisfied that it had been a perfect Christmas, with their friends, daughter and son-in-law and baby granddaughter.

23

MORE LETTERS ...
JANUARY TO JUNE 1888

St James Student House,
St James Street,
Kilmainham,
Dublin
Saturday 7th January 1888

DEAREST LOUISA AND CHARLES,

I cannot believe how fast our holiday at home passed. It seemed like we were just off the ferry from Dublin then we were on it going back again. The return sailing was not nearly as unpleasant, as mercifully, the Irish Sea wasn't as rough.

It was lovely to be able to spend so much time with you and baby Evangeline. She really is quite advanced for her age and I predict that she will be top of her class in all subjects, when she goes to school.

We have all settled in again in our student house. We're going over last term's work just to refresh our memories and so we're not lagging behind when lectures recommence on Monday.

I must say this to you both, it was wonderful to be home,

but I am very excited about the new term, ready to embrace the academic studies, but I'm also very much looking forward to doing something practical to help the poor in Dublin, especially the women and children. Do you remember the volunteer work that I'd said Juliette and I had signed up for? Well, we have a start date of next Saturday, that's the 14th. We will receive initial basic training and orientation. The organisation is called "The St Vincent de Paul Society", run by the Catholic Church and is a social work and community-based service for the poor. I believe there are local branches in all parts of the United Kingdom.

Well my dears, I shall close here and post this on my way into town. We are having a day out since this will be my last free Saturday in a while.

Sending you all love and kisses, as always,
 Your loving sister, Letty xx

4 Hatton Place,
 Edinburgh,
 Monday 2nd April 1888

Dearest Letitia
 Can you believe our darling Evangeline had her first birthday last week? We had a little celebration at home with both sets of grandparents. Mrs Hammond baked a lovely cake and we all helped Evangeline to blow out her candle. Of course, she did not really understand what it meant, only that it was a special day with presents and a cake. She received so much attention that I am afraid she might end up spoiled. She is such a contented little

girl with a sunny disposition. Your mother said she takes after her father, who was a happy and adorable child.

We went to John Patrick Photographers in Morningside to have our portraits taken. We had a family group first of all, then one of Evangeline on her own. I am enclosing copies for you Letty, but please don't laugh at the family one. We had to stay still for such a long time, I ended up looking like I have a nasty smell under my nose! Charles and Evangeline are natural photographic subjects as you can see. Isn't Evangeline's little dress beautiful? I love the blue satin sash - of course you won't be able to tell what colour it is from the black and white photograph!

How are you getting on in your studies and how is your volunteer work going now? Do you enjoy it? I hope you're not overdoing things Letty, with your university work and helping the poor. Please take some time each week for social meetings with friends, it's not good to work, work, work all the time.

Charles is as busy as ever these days, but he always enjoys reading your news. He said he wasn't surprised to hear about the volunteer work, you're a very kind and caring woman. We are all looking forward to seeing you after your end of year examinations, which must only be a couple of months away now.

I shall close this letter here Letty dear and get those photographs off to you this afternoon. Please take care of yourself and give my warmest regards to the others.

With love from us all, your sister-in-law and friend,

Louisa xx

ST JAMES STUDENT HOUSE,

Dublin,
Sunday 27th May 1888

Dearest Louisa and Charles,

This first year in medical school has flown by so quickly, I can hardly believe we're about to sit our first year examinations. We have all been studying really hard, even on Saturday mornings, so I'm doing only a half day for the St Vincent De Paul Society until after our our examinations.

I am so sorry that what I am about to tell you will be a disappointment to you, as I know it will be to Mother and Father. I have decided to spend the summer vacation in Dublin. I have secured an appointment at the Rotunda Hospital, which is a maternity hospital for the poor of Dublin. The experience that I shall get there, working with specialists in Obstetrics, will be invaluable for my future practice in medicine.

Louisa, you asked me about my volunteer work. Well it's very hard to describe the living conditions of the people St V de P helps. The slums here, I believe from what I've been told, are worse than those in London, Glasgow and Birmingham.

After our initial training, Juliette and I were taken to the street where the people we were to work with live. In this street Louisa, there are over one thousand people in one hundred households. They all live in just 16 houses. The houses were built for the wealthy in the Georgian era, but have long been abandoned and are now tenanted by the poorest of the poor. Most of the households are run by women, who are either widowed or single.

You wouldn't believe the conditions in which these women struggle to make homes for their families. Why is it always the women who bear the brunt of poor and inadequate housing Louisa? They are cooking over open fires, carrying water up several flights of stairs and have to organise the space so as to keep some level of privacy. The ceilings are high and it's impossible to keep the draughty rooms warm in winter. Individual rooms are occupied by between three and ten people, so you can imagine how difficult it must be in terms of privacy and personal hygiene practices. Our housemates were horrified the first few times we returned home from the slums, since we went straight to the bathroom and removed all our clothes, piece by piece, and shook them over the bath to get rid of any lice we picked up during our visit to the poor.

Upon my word, we don't know how fortunate we are. It's as though we inhabit completely different worlds. However, now that I have seen, first hand, how the poor live, I will never forget it and I shall never be complacent about my privileged life. These conditions prevail even when the breadwinner is employed. My heart goes out to those people Louisa and I feel so helpless, as anything I could contribute (in terms of food etc) would only be a "drop in the ocean" and I know that what the situation requires is a complete redistribution of wealth in society, which I doubt will ever happen, as greed and the accumulation of wealth is what motivates a lot of the people who govern the United Kingdom. The child and maternal mortality rates are extremely high, and this, along with the poverty I witness here, is what led me to thinking about working at the Rotunda over the summer.

I will be home for two weeks in September for a short holiday, before we begin second year at the beginning of October. I am sure I shall have lots to talk about to you and Charles then and I can't wait to see Evangeline, who I imagine will be talking by then.

The six of us are thinking of finding a house to rent for our second and subsequent years, now that we have found our feet in Dublin. We have managed to get on really well with us all sharing a dormitory, with just the occasional disagreement, and we think it will work out well. Wish us luck in finding a suitable place to rent.

That is all my news for now, please kiss Evangeline for me. Sending lots of love to you and Charles too.

As always, your loving sister,

Letty xx

24

PERILS OF THE DUBLIN SLUMS
SATURDAY 27TH OCTOBER 1888

The women were well settled in the house they were renting, which wasn't far from the student house and also on St James Street, which meant they could easily walk the distance to the hospital and lecture rooms.

Letty and Juliette had been volunteering with the St Vincent de Paul Society for nine months now and they had formed a good relationship with the clients they went out to see each Saturday afternoon. They soon learned that after visiting the poorest in Dublin, they had to go straight to the bathroom on their return, strip off all their clothing and shake them in the bath to clear them of any lice picked up. They then washed the lice away down the drain. The other housemates were horrified at first, but they soon got used to the routine and made sure the bathroom was free for Letty and Juliette to delouse in as soon as they got home.

It had been emphasised in their training that they must only go out in pairs. "If, for some reason, your partner cannot go, then under no circumstances is any one woman to go on her own," their trainer had said sternly. This particular day however, Juliette had come down with a very bad cold and was confined to bed. It came on suddenly over the Friday night and it was too short notice for Letty to arrange for someone else to go with her.

Letty was in two minds whether to risk it and go on her own. She said as much to Juliette.

"No Letty, you mustn't go on your own. You know the rules," croaked Juliette, who had a sore throat and was almost hoarse.

"I know Juliette, but there has never been a sign of trouble all the times we have been there, I shall be fine," replied the stubborn Letty, "besides Mrs Reilly is depending on us visiting, she may have had the baby by now and will need my help. Little Seamus is only ten months old, so she'll have two babies on her hands."

She had worn Juliette down, which, in her current condition, wasn't difficult. "Alright, but take one of the others with you and make sure you're home before it gets dark," she said, bursting into a violent bout of sneezing.

Letty knew that the others had all gone to a matinee at the theatre, but said nothing to Juliette who had obviously forgotten as she was feeling so ill. "Alright Juliette. Bye now, stay warm." Then she pulled on her coat, hat and gloves, checked she had enough money for "emergencies" in her reticule and left the house.

It was around two-thirty when Letty knocked on the second floor door of Mrs Reilly's "house". The voice inside called, "Come away in girls, the door's open. I've been expectin' yous."

Letty opened the shabby door that had hardly any paint on it and went into the dim room. Mrs Reilly was one of the "lucky ones" as she had a large room which was divided by a curtain to create separate bedroom space for the older girls who were eleven, twelve and thirteen years old. Mr Reilly was an unskilled labourer who worked in one of Dublin's many breweries and seemed to take half of his pay in beer, for he never brought home enough money to feed his growing family.

In the living room, which doubled as a bedroom for Mr and Mrs Reilly and their four younger children, Mrs Reilly was sitting on a low bed suckling her new baby.

"Ah, so you've had the new baby!" Letty exclaimed, "is it a boy or a girl?"

"Tis another colleen I'm sorry to say Letty. There's not much o' a life ahead o' this wee one, to be sure."

Letty looked at the scrawny baby and her heart went out to her and her frail mother. "When was she born and do you have a name for her yet?" asked Letty, stroking the small red face, who seemed angry at her mother's insufficient milk. Her little fists flailed, as though she was complaining and fighting against the poor circumstances she had been born into.

"She's called Niamh, after me sister and she was born on Tursday," said the exhausted woman, rocking back and forth.

Just then Letty heard a whimpering in the corner and Mrs Reilly said, "Could ye see to Seamus please Letty, he doesn't seem well today and he's having trouble catching his breath. I think it must be the croup."

Seamus, who was a baby himself, was indeed having trouble. Letty took off her coat and lifted the little boy onto her knee. She realised then that the child was wet and without making a fuss, she took a grey coloured napkin drying on the fireguard, next to a badly smoking and pathetically small fire, and set about changing him. Do you have enough milk for Seamus too?" Letty asked, as she walked about with the sick child.

The woman shook her head sadly, bowed down with the weight of her circumstances. "To be sure, I don't. I've been giving him water wit a wee bit o' sugar in it, but it doesn't satisfy the wee soul, don't ye know."

Letty said, "I think you're right and Seamus does have croup. I'll get some water boiling first of all, do you have any Ipecac?"

"I've nottin' like that in the house at all," said the anxious woman, referring to the split room as "the house".

The little boy's hoarse and laboured breathing was filling the room, and he was feverish and whimpering piteously. It seemed an age before the small amount of water boiled on the poor fire, which was what Mrs Reilly used for cooking.

Letty placed a pot of hot water on the table and put a towel over the child's head so he could breathe in the steam. After about forty-five minutes, with the help of the oldest girl heating the water to keep the steam going, Seamus's breathing was only marginally improved. Letty put the child on the bed, behind his mother and said, "I'm going to run to the nearest chemist to get some Ipecac and if that doesn't work I'm afraid he might need a doctor or the hospital."

"Ah now Letty, I don't have any money for medicines or doctors," said Mrs Reilly.

"Don't worry about the money, I'll see to that," replied Letty and she put on her coat and ran from the room.

She found a chemist a couple of streets away and bought a bottle of Ipecac and breathed a sigh of relief that they had it in stock and she hurried from the shop. It was deep dusk by now and she was so distracted thinking about Seamus that she didn't hear the footsteps behind her.

A hand suddenly grabbed her from behind. "Give us yer bag Missus!" a coarse voice said and she struggled to hold onto it, her only thought was that she had to get the medicine to Seamus.

There was a foul stench of stale beer close to her face. The next thing she knew was that she was being dragged backwards into a dark alley between the houses, close to the Reilly's tenement. Still she struggled to hold on to her bag and the precious medicine for the sick child. She was pulled down onto the hard, slimy cobblestones and her assailant delivered a vicious kick to the side of her head. She lost consciousness and the bag with the baby's medicine. Before running off into the darkening evening, her assailant kicked her in the ribs, for good measure.

BY SIX O'CLOCK in the St James Street house, the theatre goers had returned and Juliette was fretting since Letty was long overdue.

"We're not meant to go there on our own, but Letty said she'd ask one of you to go with her. I'd forgotten you had all gone out for the afternoon. This blasted cold is addling my brain," she moaned, very close to tears.

"Alright Juliette, what's the address of this place where she went?" Marion asked. "Victoria and I will go to the police and Jessica and Emmeline should stay with you." She noted down the address and added, "If Letty returns after we've gone, get a message to the police." They hurried out into the dark night.

LETTY BEGAN to come round and she wondered where she was and what she was doing laying on the cold, damp ground. Then she remembered what had happened and she tried to get up. As soon as she raised herself up she began to feel nauseous and her head was spinning. With excruciating pain in her ribs, she slowly rolled over and struggled onto her knees. She knew if she vomited whilst on her back, she could choke.

She was drifting in and out of consciousness for what seemed like an age when she became aware of someone bending over her and speaking to her. "Is your name Letitia Frobisher Miss?" She cowered, thinking her attacker had come back and the voice spoke again, "I'm a constable Miss and I'm going to get help." He gave a short blast on his whistle and, a few moments later, another constable arrived, followed a few minutes later by Marion and Victoria.

The next thing Letty knew was that Marion and Victoria were kneeling down and looking her over to assess her injuries in the light of the lanterns the constables were holding up.

In faltering gasps Letty said, "I have cracked or broken ribs - broken I think and my head is pounding where he kicked me." Marion and Victoria looked at each other in horror, then Marion checked her pulse which was strong but erratic.

"We need to get her to hospital immediately," she said to the policemen, "we can't risk her broken rib puncturing her lung. This is an emergency!"

"My bag," rasped Letty, "the medicine was in the bag. Child needs it … afraid he'll die."

"We'll arrange for him to go to hospital," Marion reassured her friend and she asked one of the constables to see to that while they got Letty herself to the hospital. He hurried off to the Reilly home to get the child and take him to the children's hospital in Upper Temple Street.

An hour earlier Marion and Victoria had arrived at the police stationed and they insisted that they go with the constables as Letty might need their help. The constables agreed and they all travelled in a police wagon to 16 Buckingham Street, the address where the Reillys lived. The constables began searching the area while Marion and Victoria went to see Mrs Reilly,

"Your one, Letty," she said, "she went to the chemist to get some medicine for Seamus. He's got the croup, don't ye know now, and the steam didn't work, so she hurried out and I'm that worried about her and the child too," said Mrs Reilly, almost without taking a breath, "Sure I don't know what I'm to do wit' the wee soul."

They took one look at Seamus and they knew he was in a bad way. Victoria said, "Mrs Reilly, he needs to go to the hospital right away, we'll arrange for him to go as soon as we can." At that moment they heard the urgent blast of a police whistle from the street outside and they rushed out, fearing the worst.

25

LETTY IS ADMITTED TO HOSPITAL

Satisfied that Seamus was being taken care of, they now turned their attention back to Letty. "How are we to get her up without causing further damage?" Victoria asked, looking extremely worried.

"Well we have to do something, and quickly," replied Marion. Then she said to Letty, "do you think you could get up with our help if I wrap my jacket around you to help stabilise your rib cage Letty love?"

"Yes" gasped Letty.

Marion took off her jacket and, as gently as she could, she tied it around Letty. Suffering agonies, she allowed her friends to help her up with much wincing and cries of pain. With slow painful steps they got her to the wagon and now the problem was how to get her into it without hurting or damaging her further.

It was a slow and agonising journey to the hospital, over the cobblestones, even though the constable did his best not to jolt the wagon. Letty passed out from the pain, even though she was wedged between Victoria and Marion to avoid moving more than necessary. The nearest hospital was the Rotunda where Letty had worked over the summer. With great care she was lifted out of the wagon, laid on a trolley and wheeled into the hospital.

A doctor was sent for immediately while Marion gave the treatment room nurse Letty's personal details and what she assumed had happened to Letty. From what Mrs Reilly told them and from the little Letty was able to tell them herself, it was obvious she had been robbed and viciously attacked. "Tut, tut," said the nurse, "what is this city coming to when angels of mercy are attacked in the street? I'm sure I don't know."

When the doctor arrived Letty had regained consciousness and he immediately ordered laudanum to be given to Letty before he would carry out a complete physical assessment. "I seem to know your face my dear," he said, "have you been here before?"

Knowing talking was painful for her, Victoria answered for Letty. "She worked here over the summer as a ward assistant." The doctor looked at the notes the nurse had prepared and recognition dawned on him. "Of course, the wee Scottish lass! Hello Miss Frobisher, you may remember me, I'm Dr Sheehan."

Letty nodded feebly just as the nurse returned with the painkiller. I'll give that a few minutes to begin to take effect and in the meantime, can you tell me what happened to you?"

Marion told him about Mrs Reilly and then Letty managed to speak with some difficulty because of the pain of just breathing. "I was taking ... medicine and a man," she stopped for several moments, "took my bag and ... kicked in head and ribs." Exhausted from the effort she closed her eyes. She began to feel the pain in her head and ribs easing a bit from the medicine, which she was glad of, as the doctor carefully loosened her clothing and examined her ribs. Then he looked at her head. There was a small cut where her head had struck the cobbles.

After careful examination, he said, "You have two broken ribs and I suspect concussion from the kick to your head. We will strap up the ribs and then you'll be admitted to Ward 6. Your ribs will heal in time, about six to eight weeks, I would say. Once on the ward, we will monitor you until you recover from the concussion. Hopefully there will be no tissue damage, but we'll keep an eye on you over the next thirty-six hours. The skull is pretty tough, so hopefully you have sustained only the concussion." He smiled reassuringly at the two friends. "Don't worry too much, we will keep her as free of pain as possible. What she needs now is rest."

Victoria and Marion kissed Letty gently and said goodbye. "May we visit her tomorrow doctor?" asked Marion.

"Visiting is from three to four," he said, then went to give his report to the constable.

BACK AT THE house in St James Street, Victoria and Marion gave Juliette, Emmeline and Jessica the full story of what had befallen Letty. "Poor Letty," said Juliette, "if only I hadn't had this bothersome cold I would have been with her."

"In that case," said Marion, "it might have been you Juliette. Think about it, you both wouldn't have gone for the Ipecac, one of you would have stayed there with Seamus."

"Yes, I suppose you're right," replied Juliette.

"Anyway, we may go and visit Letty tomorrow. I'm sure she'll be feeling much better by then, well apart from her ribs, of course."

. . .

Next day, they were delighted to see that Letty was sitting up in bed and she was looking a lot better than when Marion and Victoria left her the previous evening.

Juliette reluctantly stayed at home, as the others said she must not take her cold into the hospital and maybe spread it to the sick women there.

"Oh Letty, you are looking so much better," said Victoria.

"I actually feel a lot better. I think the concussion has finally gone, although I still have a dull headache," she replied.

"We're not surprised," said Jessica, "after what that criminal did to you. I hope the police catch him and lock him up."

"How are your poor ribs now?" Marion asked.

"They're still painful when I move, but they're well strapped up and that helps a lot," she said. "But listen, please don't mention this to your families in Edinburgh. If Father hears of it, he'd come over in person and take me home. You know how he felt about me coming here."

"We promise," Jessica said on behalf of them all, "and when we get back we'll tell Juliette not to mention it either."

"Thank you. I'm not even going to tell Charles and Louisa, at least, not until I've graduated, but maybe not even then."

"Have they said when you might be discharged yet?" asked Victoria.

"Dr Sheehan is pleased with my progress and thinks maybe Tuesday or Wednesday, so I will miss lectures for a few days. Will you take notes for me please?"

"Of course we will," they all said at the same time.

The visiting hour was soon up and they gently kissed Letty on the cheek and left the busy ward.

By the time the Christmas vacation came around, Letty had made a full recovery and nobody at home suspected anything had happened to her, although she was still careful when sneezing or coughing, since her ribs still felt slightly tender.

26

LOUISA PARTS COMPANY WITH THE EDINBURGH CHILDREN'S REFUGE
AND BEGINS NEW VENTURES, 1889

During Evangeline's baby years, Louisa continued to do a limited amount of work for her Refuge at 142 High Street, as well as the two children's houses in Stockbridge. Louisa had opened a day nursery in 1880 and had followed this by opening a refuge where children, who were rescued from dire circumstances, could be looked after until more suitable, permanent places could be found for them.

After her abduction and rescue in 1885, Louisa had promised Charles that she would step back from the day-to-day running of the homes and let a manager and board of directors be responsible for overseeing her work.

In 1889, the Board of Directors held negotiations with the Glasgow Society for the Prevention of Cruelty to Children, and the two organisations merged to become the Scottish National Society for the Prevention of Cruelty to Children (SNSPCC. In later years it would become the RSSPCC, when it was granted the Royal Charter).

It was at this time that Louisa withdrew her soon-to-be redundant services, satisfied that "her children" were in safe hands. The organisation had outgrown her and she happily stepped down, confident that she had made a world of difference to the lives of the children who had passed through her homes for almost two decades.

1889 was also an important year as that was when the first Prevention of Cruelty to Children Act was passed, enabling children's societies and the police to charge those guilty of cruelty and neglect.

Louisa, who had always taken a holistic approach in her dealings with her children, had been hoping that the Act would have included mental cruelty as well, since it was not covered by any legislation so far. During her many years working with abused, abandoned and neglected children, she was acutely aware of the mental and emotional affects that ill treatment had on them.

As Evangeline got older, Louisa had more free time. She gave some of this time to the suffrage movement and had accepted an offer to serve on the committee of the Edinburgh Women's Suffrage Association, after she had stepped down from her Refuge work.

Ever since her involvement in exposing the illicit trade in young girls in 1885, Louisa recognised that there was a need for the victims of such crimes to have a dedicated female counsellor to whom they could be referred for help in dealing with the aftermath of such serious crimes.

With this in mind, in September of that year she approached the Edinburgh Police Force and arranged a meeting with Superintendent Beaton to discuss her setting up such a service in the High Street police station.

Superintendent Beaton had been an Inspector and the man in charge of *Operation Stealth*. He and his team of policemen were responsible for closing down the highly organised trade in child prostitution in Edinburgh and Glasgow, putting the perpetrators in prison for a very long time.

His contribution to the success of the operation was rewarded by promotion to the rank of superintendent.

"Good morning Lady Moncrieff," he said as Louisa was shown into his office, "it's a pleasure to see you again." As an inspector, he had always been confused as to how she should be addressed and Louisa had never corrected him when he used her mother's title when talking to her.

Holding out her hand to shake his, she said kindly, "It's Mrs Frobisher now Superintendent."

"Of course, how can I help you Mrs Frobisher?" he replied, "but first, let me order some refreshments. Tea or coffee?"

Louisa sat in a comfortable chair and they exchanged pleasantries while they waited for a constable to bring their tea.

Having poured the tea and handing a cup and saucer to Louisa, he said, "I read about the Children's Refuge merging with the Glasgow Society. I hope they serve our needy children as well as you did in your years up the road at 142 High Street."

"I am sure they will Superintendent," replied Louisa, "they have some very wealthy and highly placed patrons, so they should be assured of the funds they require for such a large organisation."

"And what brings you here today dear lady?" he asked.

"I'm here with a proposal for the Edinburgh Police," she said, sipping her tea, "You will, no doubt, remember that after the girls were rescued from Royal Terrace, I suggested that it might prove helpful for the women and girls who are the victims these sorts of crimes, if there was a woman working alongside the police, someone they could talk to about what they had experienced?" she asked.

"I do indeed, Mrs Frobisher and, at the time, I put the

idea forward to my superiors, hoping that, in the light of that case, they would accede to the request. However, the investigation of the perpetrators and liaising with the Glasgow Police was their priority at the time and I'm afraid the matter did not proceed further."

"I see," said Louisa, "in that case, may I put forward a proposition now?"

"And what is your proposition Mrs Frobisher?" Beaton asked with interest.

"I am willing to work as a counsellor, on a voluntary basis, with the women and girls who are the victims of sexual assault and rape, or indeed other serious crimes. All that I would ask of the police is that I am allocated a room, or office, where I might hold these meetings. Also, that the victims should be referred to me by the investigation officers for an initial assessment to decide if what I am offering is suitable for their needs."

Beaton listened as Louisa spoke, nodding his head in agreement with the idea. "That is a most generous offer Mrs Frobisher. I will wholeheartedly support your proposal. Would you submit it to me in writing please and I shall ask my superiors to give it their consideration."

"Thank you Superintendent Beaton, this is an issue that has concerned me since you rescued those girls. I am convinced that when physical injuries have healed, that is not the end of the trauma for those affected, especially so if the crime has been perpetrated over a prolonged period of time."

He nodded again, "And, since it won't cost the Force anything, other than letting you have the use of an office, I feel quite positive that they will make a favourable decision."

"Thank you again Superintendent, for everything."

Louisa stood up, ready to leave, and they both knew that she was also thanking him for being instrumental in her being rescued from the same place as the young girls in 1885, as well as the support for the scheme she had just proposed.

"I shall have the written proposal sent to you within the next day or so."

"Good day Mrs Frobisher, it has been a pleasure to see you again."

"Good day to you Superintendent." said Louisa.

Louisa submitted her detailed proposal in writing and was, in due course, permitted to offer a counselling service to women and young girls for a six month trial period, at the end of which, a decision would be made whether to make it permanent.

Six months later

LOUISA'S SCHEME was a huge success and was much used, with referrals from the police. She became the first woman to work for the police force in Edinburgh.

27

EDINBURGH SCHOOL BOARD, MONTHLY MEETING

WEDNESDAY 6TH NOVEMBER 1889

Major McClelland barked, "Any other business?" He was the chairman of the School Board and he wanted to bring the meeting to a close. He often forgot that he was no longer in the army, and that the Board members were not his soldiers.

His didactic manner irked Miss Flora Stevenson and a few of the progressive minds there, including Louisa Frobisher.

Louisa spoke up, "I would like to propose, under "any other business" that children in schools in the poorest areas be given a plain breakfast and midday meal, free of charge."

There was a stunned silence, followed by a rumble of murmuring around the table. Several members were expecting to have to dive for cover, metaphorically speaking, whilst others were looking forward to a heated exchange.

Major McClelland was almost apoplectic. "My dear lady," he said, through gritted teeth and emphasising the word "lady" in a condescending tone. "It is not the place of the School Board to feed children, that is the duty of the parents."

"Hear! Hear!" from some of the longest serving and most conservative members.

Unruffled by his tone, Louisa replied, "Then perhaps it should be. Many children go to school so hungry they can barely concentrate on their lessons. Some do not attend at all for the same reason."

"Perhaps if the parents spent less money on drink, they would be able to feed their numerous children," spluttered the Major.

The Board was comprised of male members with two exceptions: Miss Stevenson and Mrs Frobisher and the men were openly hostile to having female members on the Board.

Major McLelland was extremely parsimonious and Louisa was determined to get free school meals for the poorest children.

"There are many abstemious families who work for a pittance and who cannot afford to feed their children satisfactorily," retorted Louisa, colour rising in her cheeks. She abhorred this constant blaming the poor for their poverty, rather than the iniquitous social and economic conditions which prevailed.

"Stuff and nonsense!" exclaimed the chairman. "We've never bribed children to come to school in the past and I don't see any good reason why we should do so now. It would be a scandalous waste of ratepayers money."

Louisa asked, "What is the point of providing an education for children who are in no physical state to learn through lack of food?"

"Hear! Hear!" said Miss Stevenson, adding, "now *that* is a waste of money."

"Feeding hungry children to enable them to make the most of their education is not bribery," said Louisa emphatically. She looked around the table and added, "I noticed that several members of this Board were not averse to partaking of the afternoon tea provided for them at the ratepayers expense."

The Board were always served with tea, sandwiches and cakes half-way through their meeting and the same people tucked into it greedily each time.

Louisa was gratified to see some expressions of embarrassment and added, "I am not suggesting that we give the children smoked salmon sandwiches and chocolate cake, just plain, nourishing fare."

"I agree with Mrs Frobisher," said Flora Stevenson. "I have personally spoken to teachers in the poorest areas and they agree that the most difficult part of their work is trying to teach children who are unable to concentrate or who faint from hunger."

"First you ask us to provide free school meals, what will it be next - for us to clothe them?" said McClelland, warming to his argument.

Louisa and Flora looked at each other amused and by mutual, tacit consent, the latter responded.

"I'm afraid you're a bit late for that Major." He looked confused, not knowing what she meant. She continued, "I'm surprised a man in your position is not aware of the Police Fund."

"What Police Fund?" he demanded testily.

She took pleasure in enlightening him, "The Police Fund, or to give it its full name, The Police Aided Clothing Scheme which which was set up recently by the Lord Provost and the Chief Constable of the Edinburgh Police Force."

"Oh that, yes of course, it had slipped my mind momentarily," replied a rather embarrassed chairman.

Bringing them back to the subject in hand, Louisa said, "This is the second time, since I have been on this Board, that I have raised this issue and I was not permitted a proper hearing. Since then, I have undertaken some research into the costing of such a venture and ..."

Before she could finish, Mr McLeod, the treasurer, asked, "How much would it cost to feed them Mrs Frobisher?"

Louisa took a sheaf of papers from her briefcase and passed them around the table. They had all begun to look at the various estimates she had provided when the chairman interrupted. "I say," he said, "we do not have sufficient time for this. Bring it to next month's meeting!"

Miss Stevenson fixed him with a gimlet eye and asked, "How long can it possibly take, Mr Chairman, to peruse Mrs Frobisher's findings? As you will see, if you care to look at it, she has done all the hard work already." She did not want the momentum gained to be lost by leaving the matter to cool for a month.

The Major had always been a little afraid of the formidable Miss Stevenson, a woman who was neither impressed nor intimidated by his title. He flushed, blinking at her and she added, "As I recall, the meeting in March lasted three hours when we were discussing what an appropriate gift would be to honour the headmaster who was about to retire from a school in one of the better-off parts of the city."

McClelland looked discomfited and said in a resigned tone, "Go on Mrs Frobisher."

Louisa spoke eloquently and succinctly about the benefits of providing meals for the children and the disadvantages of not providing them, for both teachers and children. They discussed it for half an hour and Miss

Stevenson contributed observations from her own enquiries.

Finally, it was put to a vote. The chairman said, "All those in favour of feeding the children, raise your hand." His own hand remained at his side. "All those against ..." he raised his hand and was dismayed that the majority had voted to provide free school meals to children in the poorest areas. Those against were narrowly defeated by two votes.

"Motion passed," said a disgruntled chairman and he added, "now may I call this meeting to an end?"

There were replies of "of course" as the members filed out of the Board Room.

Since 1882, women were permitted to vote in municipal elections and to stand as candidates for the School Board. That is, if they met the property qualifications. Many women, even wealthy ones, did not qualify if they did not own a property or pay rates. An example of this group would be those still living with their parents.

When Louisa and Charles married in 1886, a house was bought for them by both sets of parents and both Louisa's and Charles's names were on the deeds to the property, as joint owners. Although the Married Women's Property Act (1870) gave women the right to keep any property they owned before their marriage, they did not have joint ownership of their husband's property.

Before this Act, everything a woman owned before marriage, immediately belonged to the husband as soon as the minister pronounced them "man and wife". This had serious consequences for women who were at the mercy of violent and controlling husbands and who had vowed to "obey" their husbands as part of the marriage ceremony. They had no means to leave and live elsewhere, so many women were forced to remain in circumstances where domestic and sexual abuse happened behind closed doors.

In January 1889, a seat had become vacant on the Edinburgh School Board due to the death of one of its members. Louisa, who had long been concerned for the welfare of children, campaigned with help from her family and friends for election onto the Board and won the seat. She was only the second woman to take her place on it. The other was Miss Flora Stevenson, who was a seasoned campaigner for women's rights and a founder member for the Edinburgh Association for the higher education of women.

Louisa had a strong ally in Miss Stevenson. In fact, it was she who encouraged Louisa to stand for election. She was a contemporary of Louisa's mother and they had both joined the suffrage movement at its inception in 1867. Both women's contribution to the School Board made a substantial impact on the lives of Edinburgh's poorest children. For many, it was the only nourishing food they got all day and, in addition to improving concentration, it was an incentive to attend school.

Over a period of time, from her work with female victims and her experience on the School Board, Louisa became acutely aware of how powerless women were in such a male-dominated society and how important it was, in the first instance, that women should be granted the franchise. She was not naive enough to think that the vote would remove the many inequalities between men and women, and there would be many more battles ahead, but having the vote would be a good start.

28

LETTERS FROM LETTY
DUBLIN 1891

Letty was coming to the same conclusion in Dublin.

15 St James Street,
  Dublin.
  12th January 1891

Dearest Louisa and Charles,
Here I am back in the thick of it again, at the beginning of our penultimate term. Can you believe that we are in our final year already? It doesn't seem like three years ago when we were living in the student house.

It is so much better having our own house and having the independence to come and go as we please without asking for a late pass. I think we are all old enough - much older than most of our fellow students who were fortunate enough to come here straight from school - to not be foolish and distracted from our studies. These places were so hard-won that we are making the most of the opportunity.

Most of the final two terms will be spent on the wards, honing our clinical skills and preparing for the examination in our clinical practice. Our tutors are excellent clinicians and encourage us to learn by example. I personally blossom from this approach, preferring the carrot to the stick, as the saying goes. I can't imagine Professor Pilkington, in the Edinburgh Medical School, using that approach. Can you Charles? I would say that man is happier with a stick, or whip, in his hand and I don't think he has a humane bone in his body. We are really so much better off here. Edinburgh could learn a lot from the way they do things in Dublin, inclusive as opposed to exclusive. I think Professor Pilkington would be rather cross if he realised he had actually done us a great service.

Louisa, you are doing such good and important work, both on the School Board and with the female victims of crime. You really are pioneering new ideas and the longer I work with the poor, the more I am coming to the conclusion that just getting the vote will not be enough. There are so many inequalities suffered by women and so many other rights to be won, that I fear we may may still be campaigning when we are as old as our mothers are now. I hope not, but I think we have a long battle ahead of us. However, I am a pragmatist and gaining the franchise will be the first and necessary step on the long journey to equal rights.

Thank you both for an utterly delightful time over Christmas. It was wonderful to spend so much time with you and I couldn't believe how grown up Evangeline was. I hadn't seen her since Easter with working at the Rotunda during the summer vacation. Upon my word, she is a proper little girl now. She is very articulate and has a wide vocabulary and is very clever for her age. I just loved her "reading" me bedtime stories! Being in the nursery class has really brought her on. I am looking forward to coming back to Edinburgh later in the year, so I can see more of you both and get properly reacquainted with my beautiful and bright goddaughter.

I must close here and prepare for tomorrow's lectures. The weather remains cold here and very damp.

Sending you all much love and kisses,
    As always, your loving sister,
    Letty xx

15 St James Street,
    Dublin.
    18th March 1891

Dearest Louisa and Charles,

First of all, allow me to apologise for being a bad correspondent of late. Thank you for your regular letters which keep me up to date with what's happening at home and, of course, Evangeline's, always interesting, comings and goings both at home and in the nursery.

I have been frightfully busy studying as much as I can during this very important term. I have, reluctantly, cut back on some of the hours at the St Vincent de Paul Society until after the final examinations in June, but since I will be here over the summer until graduation and taking my licence examination, I shall be able to give them much more time then.

Charles, you will be delighted to hear that I passed the clinical exam yesterday and this counts towards my degree, so it was really important that I did well. It was rather nerve-wracking as all the others to date have not counted towards the final.

The timing of it was most fortunate since we were all able to attend the St Patrick's night Ball at the university. The Irish really celebrate St Patrick's Day and every one of the Edinburgh Six attempted Irish dancing, which was quite a feat, I must say! We were all in excellent spirits after our exams and had a wonderful time.

I'm sorry I won't be with you for Evangeline's birthday on the 25th so I am enclosing a little gift for her. I can hardly believe she is going to be four years old, please remember me to her and give her a big kiss and cuddle from Aunt Letty.

I'm sending you all my love and best wishes for a wonderful time on Evangeline's birthday.

Your loving sister,
   Letty xx

4 HATTON PLACE
WEDNESDAY 25TH MARCH 1891

"Happy Birthday Evangeline!" said Grandmama and Grandfather Moncrieff.

It was Evangeline's fourth birthday and she was greatly excited by the occasion. Both sets of grandparents were there and, of course both her parents as Charles had taken some time off work. Uncle George was now working in a mission in China and had sent her a beautiful doll. Aunt Letty was studying in Dublin and had sent her a silver bangle which could be adjusted to fit her wrist as she got older.

"Your grandfather has brought you a special present," said Grandmama Moncrieff, "come into the vestibule sweetheart, and see what it is."

Wondering what it could be, she followed her grandmother out of the drawing room and into the vestibule. Everyone else there was in on the surprise. Her grandfather was standing beside a shiny new tricycle built especially for her [by the Leicester Safety Tricycle Company]. It was painted dark green with gold curlicues and it had a little compartment on the back with the letters "EF" in beautiful script. On the front was a little wicker basket and brass bell.

Delight followed a momentary stunned surprise and she clapped her hands with joy. She stroked the handlebars, which had gold coloured ribbons tied to them, then she walked slowly around it. When she reached the back she stopped and clasping her little hands with pleasure, she pointed to her initials. "Look everyone, it says Evangeline Frobisher!" She already knew the alphabet and her own name.

"Well," said Lord Moncrieff, happy to be the bringer of such joy to his granddaughter, "perhaps your mother and father will take you out on it. In the meantime, you can get plenty of practice on the path around the house."

Evangeline looked at her parents, "Would you Mother, Father?" She was now sitting on the tricycle, trying out the bell.

"Of course we will," said her mother, answering for both of them, "and you may also cycle around the houses on the pavement when Maggie has time to take you." Maggie was the housemaid who had replaced Gertie when she married two years before. She was also one of the girls rescued from Royal Terrace in 1885.

Evangeline was a sweet-natured child and was adored by her family and friends, much like her father was as a child. Despite being the only child in the family, she was not spoiled in any way. She had a fair complexion, with the same striking blue eyes and auburn hair as her mother, which she wore in ringlets, usually tied with blue ribbons that matched her eyes. Her father called her his "princess" and was very proud of her. She had the same caring nature of her father and the determination of her mother, which sometimes led to a battle of wills if she wanted to do something her own way.

Since Harvey had gone to his canine heaven the previous year, the family had got a new companion for their young daughter. This latest addition to the family was called Matilda and had arrived when she was a little black and white bundle, a sweet greyhound puppy, with blue eyes and floppy ears.

Like her mother when she was young, Evangeline talked to Matilda as though she understood what was being said to her and, at times, it seemed like she did. At four years old, she still remembered the large, gentle deerhound cross, who had been her mother's companion for many years. She had heard the stories of how Harvey went to work every day with her mother to the Children's Refuge and how he was loved by all the children and nurses there. He was even well known at the police station in the High Street, as they often took children to the Refuge to be looked after. The whole family mourned Harvey's passing; he was a devoted, gentle giant and Louisa still missed hime sorely.

As with her parents and grandparents before her, Evangeline was being brought up in a family with progressive views and who believed the same opportunities should be open to girls and women that boys and men already enjoyed. This included equal access to university education and, of course, the parliamentary franchise.

Evangeline's nanny had been carefully chosen for her ability to stimulate the child's mind and to encourage independence. By the time she was old enough to go to school, she would have a good basic foundation in reading and counting.

Louisa and Charles had already decided that she would be enrolled in the same private school in Queen's Street that her mother and Aunt Letty had attended, The Edinburgh Ladies College, which taught girls from five to seventeen years of age.

Charles and Louisa watched their daughter engaged in animated conversation with the adults in the room and both felt immense pride and affection. Evangeline was confident without being precocious and had an innate knowledge of her place in the world. They sometimes wondered whether this had anything to do with the traumatic and dramatic way she had arrived in it.

They looked at each other and knew they were thinking the same thing. They felt blessed that Louisa had survived the near fatal haemorrhage when Evangeline was less than three months old. Charles had vowed, during his long vigil with Louisa, that he would never put her life at risk like that again. There would be no more babies and he had been true to his word.

Louisa remembered the conversation she'd had with Charles in the July of that year, once she was fully recovered. He had explained to her that she had almost died due to the delayed complications following Evangeline's birth. Louisa had been totally dismayed.

"Louisa my dear," he had said, holding both her hands in his, "giving birth is fraught with many dangers to a woman's life."

"Oh Charles," she'd wept, "I wanted so much to have three or four children. I don't want Evangeline to grow up as an only child like I did."

Charles spoke with great sympathy, "I know that and it pains me to disappoint you, but I would rather have only Evangeline and her mother alive, than four children with no mother to love them and watch them grow."

Louisa had reluctantly agreed, although she missed the

former physical closeness with Charles, but she knew it was the right and the safest decision.

Charles had looked at her sad face and asked, "What is it Louisa? Is there something else troubling you?"

"Oh Charles," she'd wept, "I enjoy our closeness so much, I can't imagine us not making love again."

"But Louisa, my dear," he said wiping her tears away, "we will still be able to make love. There are sheaths made from galvanised rubber which will provide a physical barrier so you won't get pregnant, I hear they are very reliable."

"Oh Charles!" she exclaimed surprised, "that's wonderful! How silly of me to forget that you would know about such things." She reflected on how satisfying their physical relationship had been since then.

Coming back to the present day Louisa called, "Evangeline, I think it's time to get changed for your party, as your friends will be arriving in a little while." She had been allowed to invite five friends to celebrate her birthday with her.

"Excuse me Grandmama," she said to Louisa's mother who was in conversation with her, "I must go now, but I shall be back soon." She skipped happily over to Louisa, took her mother's hand and they went upstairs together.

30

INCIDENT ON THE FORTH BRIDGE
FRIDAY 12TH JUNE 1891

As the one-thirty from Edinburgh to Aberdeen steamed its way across the first span of the Forth Bridge, the guard caught sight of a figure leaning over the parapet and gazing at the choppy waters of the Firth of Forth, one hundred and fifty feet below.

After standing stunned for a few moments, he hurried through the carriages to the driver's cabin and told him about the figure, possibly a young woman.

"Nowt we can do about it Jimmy, we can't stop and we can't go back. There's a goods train following us soon, so can't do owt about it lad," said the Yorkshireman who had begun his shift on the Kings Cross to Aberdeen in York, six hours earlier.

The guard turned pale with shock and said, "We cannae leave her there Bert."

"Telegraph back to Dalmeny station and tell them to fetch t'police to remove t'stupid blighter, could cause an accident." instructed Bert.

Jimmy sent the telegraph message to Dalmeny station, their last stop just before crossing the bridge. The stationmaster there alerted the police and Jimmy would have to wait until the following day to find out if the 'unfortunate', as his kindly heart thought of the person, was rescued or had jumped to a watery death.

EIGHTEEN YEAR old Rose Buchan stood clinging to the red-painted rail on the viaduct section at the south end of the Forth Bridge. She gazed down into the water below, rocking slightly, back and forth.

She was mesmerised by the clear blue of the reflected sky in its cold depths. It was a beautiful, bright, sunny afternoon and the brisk breeze whipped tendrils of hair across her face.

Rose had reached the end of her tether. Six years earlier, almost to the day, the twelve year old Rose had been given, what she and her family believed to be, the opportunity of a lifetime. She was to be maid-cum-companion to the disabled daughter of a wealthy Edinburgh merchant and she was driven away from her home, near Cramond Village, to start a new life in the great city of Edinburgh.

However, when she arrived at the big Georgian house in Edinburgh's Royal Terrace, she was informed by the housekeeper, Mrs Green, that there was no Miss Sophie. "No Miss Sophie, just men, many, many men."

Rose had written to her widowed mother every week, as she'd promised on her departure from home, but she never had a single reply to her many letters home and she thought that her family had forgotten all about her. In fact, Mrs Green had burnt the letters from home, just as she'd burnt the ones written by Rose, who believed the housekeeper was posting them each week.

In October that year, 1885, Rose and the other young girls incarcerated there, were rescued by a police raid on the premises. Rose was returned to her mother and sisters the next day, by a kind detective sergeant, and she thought that would be an end to all the trauma she had suffered.

"How naive Ah wis," she thought bitterly, "thinkin' that bein' back hame wid wipe oot a' the horror o' thae months in the Gideon Gentlemen's Club."

Although the first few weeks at home were blissful, eventually, the memories of what she was made to suffer haunted her, night and day. She became more and more withdrawn and reclusive and her mother and sisters finally stopped asking, or coaxing her, to go out with them.

Over the last four years, she'd hardly been out of the house at all, apart from her lonely wanderings, as thoughts of self-blame and self-disgust tormented her. She often thought, "Ah must have been really bad tae have been sent there. Did Ah really agree tae day such debased acts? Naw, Ah widnae. Or did Ah?" This pattern of thinking always left Rose confused.

Over the years, her perception of what had happened during those months in Royal Terrace, and her view of the world had become distorted. She had taken to walking around the countryside on her own and she spoke to her family less and less. By this time Violet and Daisy were married and only the youngest, Ivy, was still at home.

Since she refused to leave the house, but needed to earn money to contribute to the family's finances, her mother had taught her to sew and had arranged for her to do simple dressmaking and repairs, working from home. She increasingly felt that she was a useless burden to her mother and sister.

Looking down at the swirling water, she remembered

the day the Forth Bridge was opened by the Prince of Wales, the previous year. It was one of the rare times she had gone out with her family.

She remembered the scene clearly, looking up in awe at the amazing feat of engineering. Following the collapse of the Tay Bridge in the December storm of 1879, the plans for a similar bridge over the Forth were rejected and the new bridge was built to the *cantilever* design instead. It was heralded as a wonder of Victorian engineering and was the longest bridge of its kind in the world.

The image of the bridge had increasingly imposed itself upon Rose's mind over the past weeks and she'd taken to walking the five miles from home to look at the bridge.

"Well Rose, now that yer here, what are ye gonnae dae?" she asked herself, as she looked down at the water and felt her resolve waver. Suddenly, she heard men's voices and she froze. She looked round and saw two police constables approaching her.

One of them called out, "Come away from there Miss, you're not allowed on railway property."

"Dinnae come any nearer or Ah'll jump," she shouted back. She hitched up her skirt and started to put one leg over the rail. She balanced precariously on top and looked down into the water below, swaying perilously towards the outer edge of the rail.

The police stopped in their tracks. "Alright Miss, we just want to talk to you."

Rose managed to regain her balance and brought her leg back down, never taking her eyes off the two men. "Talk if ye must, but dinnae come any closer, or Ah swear, Ah'll jump," she warned them.

"You have our word," the older of the two constables

said, and added, "I'm Constable McKay and this is Constable Dalrymple. What's your name Miss?"

"Rose," she said, "Rose Buchan and Ah winnae talk tae anybody except Sergeant Wilkie at the High Street polis station in Edinburgh."

"He's a long way away Rose, talk to us. What's driven you to doing something so desperate?" asked Constable McKay.

"Ah canna tell ye, it's too terrible, but Sergeant Wilkie kens a' aboot it. Ah'll no speak tae anyone else," she repeated.

She made to get up onto the rail again when Constable Dalrymple held up a placatory hand. "Alright," he said quickly, "I'll go back to the station and get a message to him. Just get down from that rail, will you? I'll be back as quick as I can."

While Dalrymple was gone, Constable McKay tried to engage Rose in conversation. "How old are you Rose?" he asked kindly.

"Eighteen." she replied.

"I have a daughter near your age Rose, and I would want someone to help her if she was in distress like you," McKay told her and he continued in this vein until Dalrymple came back twenty minutes later.

"Right Miss," he said, looking pleased with himself as he was about to deliver good news, "Fortunately Detective Sergeant Wilkie, now Detective Inspector Wilkie, was in his office and he's on his way here," said Dalrymple. "Apparently, he remembers you," he added, wondering how a DI would know this strange young woman.

Relief spread immediately across Rose's face and Constable McKay said, "Why don't you come away off the bridge and wait for Inspector Wilkie there?" he said pointing to the south end of the viaduct which was above solid ground, rather than the choppy Forth. "There'll be trains along soon."

"No thanks," replied Rose promptly, "Ah'm fine here, you can wait along there if ye like. Ah'll wait here for Mr Wilkie, ye might be trying to trick me. Ah've been tricked enough - that's why Ah'm up here."

The two policemen looked at each other, puzzled, shrugged their shoulders and then moved along the line.

Finally, around four o'clock, and after several trains had passed, DI Wilkie came along the track and spoke to the two constables. He was told how the guard on the Aberdeen train spotted the woman and the local police were alerted.

"She refuses to come off the bridge Sir, seems to think it's some kind of trick and she won't speak to anyone but you," said McKay.

"That's understandable Constable. That lass has been to hell and back as a youngster, so I'm not surprised she doesn't trust anyone."

Rose watched as the three men talked, and hoped they weren't setting a trap, but the DI sent the constables back along the bridge and he walked towards her, where she was still clinging on to the rail.

Mike Wilkie looked a little older than Rose remembered. He was now in his early fifties with his dark hair turning grey at the temples, giving him a rather distinguished appearance. His kind eyes, Rose noticed, were the same and she knew she could trust this man.

He said, "Hello Rose, you wanted to talk to me?"

"Ah'm awfy sorry tae cause ye sae much trouble Mr Wilkie." The girls that he and his colleagues had rescued all called him "Mr Wilkie" at the time. "But Ah'm at the end o' ma tether, so Ah am," she continued, "Ah really dinnae ken what tae dae for the best."

In 1885, the (then) detective sergeant and his two detective constables had undertaken a covert operation during which they observed the comings and goings at the Gideon Club. At the conclusion of their mission, the house was raided, with staff and clients arrested and the frightened girls rescued.

Mike Wilkie smiled at the young woman who he remembered as a terrified twelve year old, "It's no bother Rose, it was actually quiet in the office, I think the criminals must be on holiday." He tried to lighten the tense situation and bring a smile to the anxious-looking woman's face. He was rewarded by her smile in return.

"Let's walk back to Dalmeny Station, perhaps we can get a cup of tea and you can tell me what this is all about."

"Aye, Ah could certainly dae wi' a cup o' tea," she replied, as she let go of the rail for the first time in two hours. Her hands were shaking now, from the tight grip she'd had on the rail.

They reached the station and the stationmaster kindly provided tea and the use of his office for Wilkie and Rose.

"You see Mr Wilkie, my family dinnae understand what Ah went through in that place. They think Ah should be a'right because Ah wis brought hame. They think it's a' over an' done wi', long ago, but it's still here," Rose pointed to her head, "and here," she pointed to her heart. "Ah dinnae understand masel' why Ah'm no' normal like Ah wis before Ah wis taken tae that wicked place."

"I know what you mean Rose, finding you all there affected us policemen, and for a long time afterwards, but it helped a bit when Galbraith got sentenced to life in prison. He will never see the outside of the Calton Gaol again."

Rose was quiet for a few moments, then said, "Ah feel like Ah've been given a life sentence tae. The horror o' what they did tae us, an' blamin' masel', it never goes away. So, Ah thought, what's the point o' livin' if it's a livin' hell?"

"Oh Rose, I'm so sorry to hear how bad it's been all this time," said Wilkie, feeling utterly helpless.

"Dae ye ken how Maggie an' the others are daein' now?" she asked, "Maybe it would help tae talk tae people that have been through it. Ah cannae tell ma family, it's just too hard."

"I don't know how they are Rose, I haven't heard anything about them, but I promise to find you some help."

He was silent for a minute and then an idea struck him. He asked, "Do you remember Dr Frobisher?" Rose nodded, embarrassed as she remembered the kind doctor who had done an intimate examination of them all, with Nurse Fairbairn holding her hand.

"Dr Frobisher's wife works with female victims of crime and I think it may be possible for you to see her, even though the crime against you happened six years ago."

"Dae ye think she will see me? Ah didnae accept the help offered at the time, Ah thought everything wis gonnae be a'right just by being hame."

"Right then, I suggest I take you home and I'll speak to Mrs Frobisher about what help can be arranged for you." He looked at his watch and added, "It might be tomorrow before I'm able to see her, but I promise you Rose, I will speak to her."

"Thank you Mr Wilkie," said Rose and she began to cry, "I remember how kind you were when you rescued us and the next day when you brought me hame."

"Let's get you home and not have your mother worrying about where you've got to, you must have been out for hours."

"Ah actually feel better now that Ah've spoken tae ye. It's

the first time since gie'in our statements that Ah've spoke aboot it."

DI Wilkie drove Rose home and explained to Mrs Buchan that Rose needed some help because of the lasting effects of what had happened to her in Edinburgh and that he was hoping to arrange something. "I'll send a message as soon as I have some news," he told them.

Rose and her mother waved to him from the door as he began the drive back to Edinburgh.

31

LOUISA AGREES TO SEE ROSE
HATTON PLACE, SATURDAY 13TH JUNE 1891

Louisa and Charles were having a rare Saturday morning to themselves with Evangeline and they were planning an afternoon walk to climb Blackford Hill. This was a favourite beauty spot of Louisa and Charles's as they had a panoramic, uninterrupted view of Edinburgh and beyond.

They were watching Evangeline on her tricycle as they talked, when a hackney cab pulled up in front of their gate. A man got out, paid the driver and then approached the house.

Louisa and Charles were on their way to the door, curious as to who their unexpected visitor might be, when Maggie, the housemaid, opened the door. She was greeting him like a long lost friend. "Hello Mr Wilkie, its good tae see ye again. Would you like me to tell the mistress that you're here?"

"Good morning to you too Maggie, how lovely to see you again. I didn't know you worked for Dr and Mrs Frobisher," said Detective Inspector Wilkie.

Louisa and Charles were looking on in amused silence

when Louisa decided she'd better rescue the inspector, otherwise Maggie would keep him on the doorstep all day chattering about anything and everything.

"It's alright Maggie," said Louisa, "we already know the inspector is here." They shook hands with him and Louisa said, "Please come into the drawing room Inspector Wilkie," then turning to Maggie said, "Maggie would you take Evangeline into the kitchen with you while we talk to Inspector Wilkie? And then, would you ask Mrs Hammond to bring us tea." Maggie bobbed a curtsy and went off to the kitchen with Evangeline.

"Have a seat Inspector," said Charles. He and Louisa sat on the armchairs on either side of the fireplace while Mike Wilkie sat on the sofa.

"It's good to see you again," said Louisa, who still felt she owed a debt of gratitude to the man who had helped to rescue her almost six years earlier, "have you come on police business?"

Although Louisa worked one afternoon a week in the High Street police station, she had not seen Mike Wilkie in passing, or otherwise.

Mrs Hammond came into the room at that moment, carrying a tray of tea and scones which she put on the side table next to Louisa. "Shall I pour for you Mrs Frobisher?" she asked. She was curious about the visitor, who she was stealing side glances at, after Maggie telling her that he had rescued her and the mistress years before.

Louisa said, "That's alright Mrs Hammond. I'll pour, thank you."

"As ye say Mrs Frobisher," she said, and taking a final look at Wilkie, hurried out of the room.

Mike spoke, "Yes, Mrs Frobisher, I am here on police business." He accepted the cup of tea Louisa offered, but politely declined the scene. "Do you remember Rose Buchan?"

Charles looked up sharply, remembering well the young girl he had examined and assessed at the Refuge in the High Street.

Louisa spoke first, "I know her name Inspector, but I didn't meet her since she'd been taken home before I went back to work the following week. I did meet the four unfortunate ones who had no home to go to, including Maggie there."

They both smiled as Maggie was always a pragmatic and optimistic girl, despite her earlier trials.

"I remember Rose," said Charles who had been rather thoughtful since Mike Wilkie had asked the question. "I remember, at the time, that I was quite concerned about her. I wasn't worried about her physical injuries, I knew that they would heal, but out of the five of them, I thought she was the most fragile mentally and emotionally."

Mike Wilkie nodded agreement and said, "Then it won't surprise you to hear what I am going to tell you."

Both Charles and Louisa listened, with concerned expressions, to Wilkie's description of the incident on the Forth Bridge and their subsequent conversation at Dalmeny Station.

"So, I have come here today to ask you, Mrs Frobisher, if you could possibly see Rose as part of your work in the High Street. I know what happened to Rose was a long time ago, but to her it feels as raw as if it was yesterday."

"Of course I will see her, if that's what she wants." replied Louisa.

"It's what she needs Mrs Frobisher and she said if I could arrange it, she would be willing to talk to you."

"Cramond is a long way from the High Street, will she be

able to get to her appointments Inspector?" asked Louisa, hoping the weekly return journey would not be an obstacle to Rose getting the help she needed.

"I think I can arrange that Mrs Frobisher. Do you remember Reverend Carmichael?" he asked her.

"Indeed I do," replied Louisa. "The man was distraught when he realised the kind of place he had delivered Rose to."

"Yes, he was suffering terrible guilt over the matter of encouraging her to apply for the job," said Wilkie, shaking his head sadly. "A constable and I went to see him after we took Rose home. Even though she was back with her family, he was still racked with guilt."

Louisa and Charles looked at him with interest, wondering what the minister had to do with it.

"I'm sure he will agree to take Rose to Edinburgh for her meetings with you and then take her home again. I think this will help lessen his feelings of guilt and it will help Rose."

"How soon can you arrange it Inspector?" asked Louisa.

"I'll drive out this afternoon Mrs Frobisher, when would you be able to see her?"

Louisa, who knew what appointments she had in her diary on Wednesday afternoon, replied, "I can see her next Wednesday, that's the 17th, at two-thirty. Ask her to report to the desk sergeant who will come and get me." Then as an afterthought occurred to her, she asked, "Has she been to Edinburgh since she returned home, do you know?"

"I very much doubt it Mrs Frobisher, she's been very much a recluse these past few years," he replied.

"In that case, I would suggest that her mother, sister or a friend should accompany her on the first journey to Edinburgh, at least."

Wilkie looked at her questioningly and she said, "If her drive to Edinburgh is with the minister only, it may feel like the time she was taken to Royal Terrace. It might induce panic in her, as though it was happening all over again. Anyone or anything that can make Wednesday's journey as different from that day will be a help."

"Of course," said Mike Wilkie, who himself remembered having a similar thought when he was driving Rose home to Cramond from Edinburgh in October 1885.

He stood up to leave and shook hands with Louisa and Charles.

"Thank you for your promise of help Mrs Frobisher. I apologise for intruding on your Saturday morning."

"Not at all," said Charles, who had liked the man when he met him while Louisa was still missing. Now, as then, the policeman's words had given him food for thought. They showed him out and said their goodbyes.

32
LATER THAT DAY
BLACKFORD HILL

Charles had been very thoughtful since their visit from Mike Wilkie. There was something niggling away at the back of his mind and it had to do with the plight of Rose Buchan, but also with other children who were mentally as well as physically damaged or injured.

They had climbed to the top of Blackford Hill and were sitting on the grass enjoying the view. To the north was Edinburgh Castle on its volcanic base, with the Firth of Forth and Fife beyond. To the east was the superb spectacle of Arthur's Seat and Salisbury Crags, and beyond that, East Lothian and the North Sea. To the west lay Craiglockhart Hill and West Lothian and to the south was the Pentland Hills and the rolling countryside of the Borders. Indeed, the other six of *Edinburgh's Seven Hills* could be seen from Blackford Hill. Evangeline was nearby, making daisy chains and Matilda was at home as she'd had a long walk earlier in the day.

"You've been very quiet since Inspector Wilkie left this morning Charles," Louisa said.

"I know my dear, I've been thinking about children who

have been victims of abuse or cruelty and how that might have an impact on their wellbeing when they are older, or perhaps the rest of their lives."

"Well it certainly seems to be the case with Rose Buchan, given what Inspector Wilkie told us." She shuddered and then said in a low voice, so Evangeline wouldn't hear, "Can you imagine feeling so low in spirit as to contemplate jumping off the Forth Bridge?"

"Exactly," said Charles, "and I've been thinking that when a child has been physically abused or ill-treated, they are suffering emotional abuse at the same time."

"How do you mean Charles?" asked Louisa.

"Especially so when it is someone they love who is inflicting the hurt or, in Rose's case, someone who is supposed to be taking care of them."

"I see," said Louisa, "Inspector Wilkie said that Rose was blaming herself."

"Yes, I think a child will try to make sense of the bad things that happen to her, or him, and will believe that they are being punished and, if they perceive it as punishment, they will very probably think they must have been naughty or have brought it on themselves somehow." replied Charles.

"I can see how that could come about," said Louisa, "rather than thinking that the all-loving, all-knowing adult is at fault, they will blame themselves."

"And possibly go through life believing they are 'bad'" said Charles. He was thoughtful for a few moments and added, "Dickens actually provides an example in *David Copperfield*, and the terrible beatings at the hands of his stepfather."

"I always found that very painful to read Charles, the cruelty to such a young child."

"He also gives an insight into the mind of a child and how they can suffer emotionally or mentally, as adults do. He demonstrates a perceptiveness of mental and emotional hurt. I think more than any of his books, *David Copperfield* has much of his own childhood in it."

"But what can be done for these unfortunate, damaged children Charles? There is no dedicated service other than the one I provide at the police station."

"I think that, with the advent of paediatrics as a separate specialism in its own right, attitudes to children, and on childhood itself, have been changing."

At that moment Evangeline, as if on cue, came up to her father and put a long daisy chain around his neck. "Thank you sweetheart," he said, "do you have one for Mother?"

"I'm going to make one for Mother now," and she skipped away to gather more daisies.

"It's not so long ago, said Charles, "that children were regarded as small, defective adults. Their innate needs were not taken into consideration in how they were treated by parents and society as a whole. Concepts of child development were non-existent. That is painfully clear in the way they were treated in the legal system, being sent to prison, or worse still, hung for stealing food. Or being sent up chimneys or working with dangerous machinery in the mill industries." He shook his head sadly.

"Is this another area that Paediatricians might become involved in, do you think?" asked Louisa.

"We already are, but only informally. Compassionate doctors and nurses pick up on the emotional or mental traumas in some of the children under our care, but there is no training in Psychiatry for children. There is no children's equivalent of the Royal Edinburgh Lunatic Asylum."

Louisa shuddered for a second time that afternoon. "The

words "lunatic Asylum" fill me with dread. I wonder how many of the patients there - I refuse to call them "inmates" - are mentally ill because of something that happened in childhood, like Rose Buchan and the others."

"We shall never know the answer to that question Louisa, unless someone decides to research into it, but academics, as far as I am aware, are not interested in lunatics, but it does give me some food for thought. Perhaps the Hospital Board would consider providing training and a service for children who are troubled."

"I think that would be a step in the right direction Charles." said Louisa, as Evangeline approached her with a daisy chain and put it around her neck.

"I think we should be heading home now ladies," said Charles, getting up from the grass, and Evangeline giggled at being classed as a lady like her mother. The three of them made their way slowly down Blackford Hill, hand in hand.

33
ROSE MEETS LOUISA
WEDNESDAY 17TH JUNE 1891

Rose was very quiet on the journey from Cramond to Edinburgh. Reverend Carmichael tried to engage her in conversation a few times and then gave up and they drove the rest of the way in silence. Mrs Buchan had gone with them, but she too, was deep in thought.

The minister was wondering whether Rose was re-living the journey with Galbraith on that far off sunny June day in 1885. He felt very uncomfortable, even guilty still, because of the part he had played in unwittingly placing Rose in such a dangerous and vile situation.

Rose wasn't thinking of that day at all. She was thinking about the meeting with Mrs Frobisher and was anxious in case she wanted Rose to go into the awful details of her incarceration in Royal Terrace.

Presently they arrived at the High Street police station and Rose and her mother got out of the minister's carriage.

"I'll be waiting here for you in an hour's time, I have some church business to attend to in the meantime."

"Thank you Reverend Carmichael," said Mrs Buchan, then she and Rose entered the police station.

As instructed, Rose gave the desk sergeant her name and said she had an appointment with Mrs Frobisher. The sergeant noted down her name. "I'll just get her Miss Buchan, please take a seat." He pointed to the other side of the room where there were chairs against the wall. Only two of them were occupied, one by a man who looked like a vagrant and the other by a worried looking woman who had seated herself as far away from the man as possible. There was a strong smell of disinfectant and the floor around the man looked like it had been recently washed.

"Ma, Ah'm gon' in masel, ye're no' tae come in wi' me, a'right?"

Disappointed because she wanted a better understanding of what had happened to Rose, Mrs Buchan replied, "A'right Rose hen, but Ah want tae meet Mrs Frobisher an' then Ah'll go an' have a walk in the Gairdens." The "Gairdens" was what the locals called Princess Street Gardens.

Relieved, Rose nodded. "When she comes for me Ah'll tell her who ye are. Ah havenae met her before masel, Ah've just met her man."

A door behind the desk opened and a well-groomed and well-dressed woman followed the desk sergeant into the reception area. The sergeant nodded towards Rose and said, "That's the lassie there Mrs Frobisher."

He lifted up the hinged part of the counter so Louisa could go over to Rose and her mother. She held her hand out to Rose first and said, "Hello Rose, I'm Mrs Frobisher."

Rose took her hand, a little embarrassed, and said, "Hello Mrs Frobisher, this is ma mother, Mrs Buchan." Her mother and Louisa shook hands and, with the introductions over, Louisa asked Rose to come up to her office. Unsure whether Mrs Buchan was joining them, she looked at her, but Mrs Buchan was already walking towards the door. "Ah'm just gon' tae have a walk, Ah'll be back in an hour Rose," she said looking at her anxious-looking daughter, feeling her pain and anxiety.

When Louisa had first started doing this work a few years before, she had bought some soft furnishings for the room. There was a colourful rug on the floor, in rich reds and blues and there was a vase of fresh flowers on her desk. It faced south, so light streamed into the room, which was situated on the fourth floor and not hemmed in by the tenement buildings nearby.

The chairs were chosen for comfort and Louisa said, "Have a seat Rose and we can have a talk and we'll see how I can help you."

Rose sat down and said, "Thank you for seeing me Mrs Frobisher. Mr Wilkie said he had told you all about me."

"He did tell me about the last time he saw you, at the Forth Bridge, the other week. I also know about what happened to you and the others six years ago. You and Bridget Kelly had gone home by the time I met the others at the Refuge." Louisa was trying to put Rose at ease and she added, "I was imprisoned in 42 Royal Terrace at the time you were rescued, but I wasn't found until the next day when Sergeant Wilkie and Inspector Beaton found me in the lower basement." Louisa hoped that, despite the obvious gap in their backgrounds and current circumstances, there might be a connection through having suffered at the hands of the same man.

Rose looked at Louisa, surprised. Louisa continued, "I was there for only two days and I did not suffer like you and the others, but I would have, I have no doubt, if Galbraith had not been arrested when he was."

Rose was again lost for words and so Louisa spoke again,

"However Rose, we are not here to talk about me. I just wanted to share the fact with you that we were both incarcerated by that callous and unspeakably wicked man." She allowed a silence of a few moments before asking, "Can you tell me Rose, what is the worst bit of it all?"

Rose was so silent and so still that she thought Rose wasn't going to speak at all. Then Rose said, "The worst bit changed over the months, if ye ken what Ah mean Mrs Frobisher."

"Can you tell me a little bit more about that please, Rose?" Louisa asked her gently.

"Well, at first like, the worst part was bein' away fae ma family an' realisin' that Ah wis locked in that hoose," she began, "an' then right away, the next worst thing wis what happened that night." Tears began to well up in her eyes as she remembered the first of countless nights in Galbraith's so-called gentleman's club.

"Honestly Mrs Frobisher, Ah really thought Ah wis gonnae die fae the awfae injuries." Rose succumbed to the emotions she had been pushing down for the past six years and sobbed uncontrollably. When she had agreed to see Mrs Frobisher, she hadn't known how difficult it would be.

Louisa went over to her and sat on the arm of the chair. She gave Rose her linen handkerchief and put her arm around Rose's shoulders. After several minutes the sobs subsided and Rose wiped her eyes and blew her nose. Louisa returned to her own chair.

"Have some water Rose," she said, pointing to the glass of water on the table next to the chair Rose was sitting in.

Rose sipped the water gratefully. "Thank you," she said, "it was something Ah could never tell ma family. Ah wis that ashamed and Ah didnae ken what they wid think aboot me if Ah could find the courage an' the words tae tell them."

"Rose, I am going to tell you something now and I will probably tell you several times throughout the course of our meetings." She regarded Rose and smiled to take away the worried look that had come across Rose's face. "It's this Rose: ***you are not to blame for what happened to you.*** The blame lies with Galbraith and the men who did those awful things to you. Do you understand what I am saying?"

Rose nodded, "Aye Mrs Frobisher. Mr Wilkie said the same thing."

"You said that the worst bit changed over time and at first it was knowing you were trapped there and then the assault on you that night. How did it change after that?"

"Well, the night thing wis always bad, but the next worse thing wis that Ah never got any letters fae ma Mammy or wee sisters, an' Ah wrote tae them every week. Mrs Green took them for posting an' Ah felt that they'd forgotten a' aboot me." The tears came again, only this time they just poured down her face silently. There were no racking sobs.

"But they hadn't Rose. Mr Carmichael came to see me in October that year because your family hadn't heard a word from you since you left with Galbraith. Your mother was worried about you. Mrs Green had been burning the letters that you wrote every week and the ones that arrived from your family. You must have felt very isolated Rose, thinking that your family had abandoned you."

Rose bowed her head, but Louisa could still see the tears falling onto her hands which were clasped tightly on her lap. She nodded again and, in a small voice, said, "If it hadnae been for Maggie and Lizzie, Ah dinnae ken what Ah wid have done. Ah sometimes thought Ah'd be better off deid an' Ah did think aboot throwin' masel off the bannister on the top flair." She was silent for a time, then said with a weak apologetic smile, "But Ah didnae, obviously."

They continued to talk about what had happened all those years ago and, for Rose, time seemed to fly by until Louisa looked at her pocket watch and said, "Our time is almost up Rose. You have gone over a lot of difficult things in the past hour, how are you feeling?"

"To be honest Mrs Frobisher, Ah feel a lot lighter than Ah have in years, if ye ken what Ah mean."

"I do know what you mean Rose."

"Ah'd been that weighed doon wi' it a' that sometimes Ah could hardly get oot o' ma bed. But efter tellin' ye aboot stuff Ah havnae tellt another soul, Ah feel like a huge weight has been lifted - no' it a', but a lot. The millstone roond ma neck feels a bit lighter. Thank you."

"If you feel it would help, you can come here every Wednesday and I will help you work your way through the remaining "worst bits" that are making up that millstone that you still feel around your neck."

"Can Ah? Please Mrs Frobisher, Ah really want tae feel better than I have these past years."

"It may feel worse before it feels better Rose but I'll be with you all the way. Think of it like you have a festering wound and the doctor needs to open the wound in order to clear out the infection, and that might be painful. But once that's done, the wound then has a better chance of healing," said Louisa.

"Yes, I can see how that would be Mrs Frobisher."

"You were very courageous to come here to meet a complete stranger to talk about extremely painful memories and experiences."

"Thank you." Rose said, a little embarrassed by being praised.

"I'll take you downstairs to meet your mother and I'll see you next Wednesday at the same time."

34

THE EDINBURGH SIX
DUBLIN, JUNE 1891

The time had come at last and the final examinations for the medical degree were taking place between Monday 22nd June and Friday 26th June. Having the letters "M.D." after their names was within their grasp.

After four years of study and clinical practice, not to mention the long years before that when they were excluded from any degree course at home, the realisation of their long-held dreams was close at hand.

All six: Letty Frobisher, Victoria Browne, Marion McNair, Juliette Whitton, Emmeline Franks and Jessica Wilmott had given up their volunteer work and social life for the entire summer term in order to concentrate on their revision and clinical practice.

They would have regular "quiz sessions" where they would test each others' knowledge of Chemistry, Physics, Anatomy and Biology. They had no lectures or clinical practice during the week before the finals, this was to allow students extra time for revision.

On the Friday before the finals, they were all sitting around the dining table conscientiously revising. The table had long since been redundant for eating meals at, and had become the centre of revision and quizzes.

This morning was no different from any other day that week and they had planned to work on into the early evening and then have the weekend off. One of their lecturers had advised against revising right up to the last minute. "I have always thought that a counterproductive practice," said Professor Kelly, "I can't stop you, of course, but my advice would be to have at least one day of relaxation before you start your examinations. Get out into the fresh air, walk along the beach or climb the hills around Dublin. Good luck to you all!"

They had all agreed to take his advice and so they were studiously occupied on their last day of revision. They had been at their books for little more than forty minutes when Marion stood up suddenly and rushed from the room, her hands covering her mouth.

The others looked up, startled. "I think she's unwell," said Victoria, "I'll go and see to her."

As soon as she left the dining room, the sounds from the WC told her what she had suspected. Marion was being violently sick. She knocked on the door and went in. Marion was leaning over the bowl and she seemed to have stopped being sick. Victoria hurried to the linen cupboard and grabbed some towels and returned to Marion.

"Marion," she said, handing her the towel, "do you think you can make it to the bedroom or are you going to be sick again?" Marion nodded her head and then clutched her stomach as a violent spasm of pain gripped her, then she was sick again. This went on for about twenty minutes - the pain and then the sickness. Marion was deathly pale and Victoria asked again if she could manage to get to her bed. Marion nodded her head and Victoria helped her up.

When they came out, the others were waiting in the hallway. They knew that their friend was ill after hearing the unmistakable sounds of retching and vomiting. Victoria asked Juliette to get a basin of water and a flannel.

By this time, Marion was shivering uncontrollably and Letty quickly took control of the situation. "I'll fetch some hot water bottles while you clean her up and get her into bed," she said. "Emmeline, will you get another basin in case she's sick again? She's in no state to be going backwards and forwards to the W.C."

They wrapped Marion up warmly in a winter nightgown and a shawl. Despite the warm spell they were having, Marion was struggling to get warm.

Whilst the others were seeing to Marion, Jessica fetched her medical bag and took out the thermometer. "Put this under your tongue Marion love," she said, as Marion sat on the edge of the bed like a limp rag, being administered to by her friends.

Jessica took the thermometer and looked at it. "She has a fever alright. Are you feeling sick Marion?" she asked and Marion shook her head. Just then Letty entered the room with the hot water bottles, wrapped in towels so they wouldn't burn her.

Emmeline had brought a jug of water and a glass, "Do you think you could take some water Marion?" and she helped her friend sip a tiny amount from the glass.

Letty said, "Let's get you settled into bed." She was shivering less now. Letty turned to the others and said, "I think we should take turns of sitting with her, for the next few hours at least, while the rest of us get on with our revision."

"I'll take the first hour," said Victoria and she sat by the bed and wrung out the flannel to put on Marion's brow. The others left the room and closed the door softly behind them.

Back around the table, they quietly discussed Marion's sudden illness. "What do you think it is?" asked Emmeline.

"Well, we're all doctors, almost, and her fever suggests she is fighting some kind of infection," said Jessica.

"I would have said it was food poisoning," said Letty, "except we have all eaten the same food this week with being at home to study. But the rest of us are well." She shrugged her shoulders, unsure what to think.

"So far," said Juliette.

"We'll keep a close watch on her today, but we may have to call a doctor if we're still worried about her this evening," replied Letty.

"I wonder if she'll be well enough for Monday's exam." Jessica had said what was in all their minds at that moment.

"We must hope so for Marion's sake," said Letty, "I know it's hard, but we must concentrate on our studies, it would be a tragedy if we did badly in our exams".

They all put their heads down and each hour the person looking after Marion would return to her studies and the next one went on nursing duty.

Victoria came into the room at five o'clock, after her second stint with Marion, just as the others were thinking about getting their supper ready.

"How is our patient now Victoria?" Jessica asked as Victoria sat down wearily.

She seems to be more feverish and is only taking tiny sips of water. I'm afraid she is becoming dehydrated," replied Victoria. "She's also fretting about the examinations next week and is worried that she won't be well enough to sit them."

"That's the decision made for us," said Letty, standing up. "I'm going to fetch Dr O'Malley. Just pray that he is at the surgery and not out on a call." She quickly put on her coat and left to walk the short distance to the doctor's practice.

She was in luck, Mrs O'Malley told Letty when she answered the door to her and Letty explained about Marion. "Sure, my husband's with his last patient now. I'll send him round as soon as he's finished."

"Thank you so much Mrs O'Malley," Letty said and she gave her the address for her husband.

"Sure that's just along the street, so it is now. He'll be with you soon."

Letty had only been back ten minutes when the doorbell rang. She opened the door to the doctor and showed him into the sick room where Marion was propped up on pillows, ready for his visit. The others stood just inside the bedroom door as he took Marion's pulse and temperature.

When he had finished his examination of her, he said, "She seems to be the victim of food poisoning. Have any of the rest of you been unwell lately?"

"No doctor O'Malley, we are all well and we wondered whether it might be food poisoning, but we've all eaten the same food all week. We've been here studying for our finals next week," replied Letty.

The penny suddenly dropped and Dr O'Malley realised that he was in the midst of the Scottish women who had come to Dublin to be doctors.

Marion's weak voice intervened. "When I was out for a walk yesterday, I bought a meat pie from the bakery and ate it on a bench in St Stephen's Green before coming back to get on with my revision."

They all looked at her in surprise. They had forgotten that she'd gone out yesterday. She'd said it was very stuffy in the house and she needed to get some fresh air, or she'd fall asleep over her books. Despite feeling so ill, Marion managed to look sheepish about not mentioning the pie before.

"Will I be well enough to sit my examiminations Doctor?" she asked. "I have to be well enough, I just have to." Tears welled up in her eyes and the doctor spoke gently and kindly, "I can't say at the moment Marion, but you must drink as much water as possible."

She nodded sadly at his lack of assurance. "However," he continued, "if you have improved over the next twenty-four hours and you are starting to take some nourishment," he looked around the others and added, "even if it's only liquids, we'll see then." He packed up his medical bag and said, "I'll come and see you again tomorrow. Good evening ladies." Letty showed him to the door and paid his fee of 2/6d. (two shillings and sixpence)

Back in Marion's room, which she shared with Victoria - both "charity girls" as they regarded themselves, it seemed natural to share the room - Marion was apologising for causing them so much trouble and disrupting their last day of revision.

Victoria said, "It's alright Marion, if we don't know it all by now, we never will."

Juliette agreed, adding, "What we really need to concentrate on now Marion, is to get you rehydrated and onto light foods." She filled the glass with water and said, "Now sip this slowly and get some rest, a good sleep will make all the difference."

By midday on Saturday Marion's temperature had returned to normal and she was able to drink some beef tea and some custard. She was still weak, but obviously on the mend by the time Dr O'Malley returned that evening.

Once again he checked her temperature and announced that he was satisfied she was beginning to recover.

"Will I be able to sit my finals next week Doctor?" Marion asked again.

"That's up to you m'dear," he said smiling reassuringly. "If you are able to eat light meals like scrambled eggs or chicken, then I don't see why not." He looked at the others and continued, "I'd say you are in good hands here and you must be guided by how you feel. Rest as much as you can until your finals and then as much as possible between each examination. Good luck to you all," he said and left the room.

Once more Letty took out the money for his fee, but he closed her hand over the coins in her palm.

"Keep your money, this consultation is free."

Thank you Doctor O'Malley, that's very good of you." replied Letty.

"Good evening Miss." he said and left the house.

ON MONDAY MORNING, a much better, but still weak, Marion joined the others and walked to the examination hall at the recently renamed Royal College of Physicians. The King and Queen's College had been given the Royal Charter and, from 1890, was known as The Royal College of Physicians.

Marion managed to do the three hour Chemistry paper, but was feeling weak and exhausted by the time noon came and she'd never been so glad to hear the Angelus bells ring.

The six friends went straight home afterwards and prepared a light meal for themselves. Afterwards they persuaded a reluctant Marion to have an afternoon nap for a few hours as it was her first day out and a big day at that.

They kept to this routine every day and gradually Marion was restored to full health. Eventually the week of examinations came to an end and the women all felt a sense of anti-climax now that their finals were over.

Emmeline said, "You know, I thought I would be euphoric when I had written the last word on that last examination paper, but I just feel flat, if you know what I mean."

"Me too," said Letty, "I thought that after four years intensive study, clinical practice and examination papers, I would be walking on air."

"I think you're forgetting an important factor ladies," said Jessica, "We are all probably physically and mentally exhausted. I'm sure our good spirits and sense of excitement will return when we go up to the college for our results."

"What we need," said Juliette, "is some fresh air and a few days out on the coast or in the countryside. Let's start tomorrow and have a few day trips, like a little holiday for our bodies and our minds."

"Agreed!" said the other five in unison.

And so, the *Edinburgh Six* kept themselves occupied and restored their flagging spirits during the sunny days leading up to the results being posted.

As hoped, and mainly expected, they all passed with good marks and, to their surprise, three of them passed with distinction: Marion, Victoria and Letty. They were all delighted and had immense fun addressing each other as Dr Frobisher, Dr McNair etc. They all loved the way it sounded as it felt very gratifying to address each other in this way.

There was one more hurdle to clear before graduation at the beginning of August and that was to pass their licensing examination, without which they would be unable to practice medicine.

. . .

This time, there was no drama and everyone was well and looking forward to completing this final step to a career practising medicine. As expected, they all passed and were licensed to practice. Their goal was at last attained, hard-won, but they had achieved it.

35

GRADUATION
DUBLIN, AUGUST 1891

Those who had suspended their volunteer work to concentrate on their studies threw themselves back into it wholeheartedly for the remaining time they were in Dublin.

Letty and Juliette were back in the slums of the inner city and were heartened to find that some of the tenants had managed to move to slightly better accommodation, either further up the same stair, or along the street to another tenement. "Better" was a relative term, when talking about housing in this part of the city, and tended to be on the upper floors since there were fewer people passing, which made it quiet, as well as having the advantage of more light in the rooms.

On a sadder note, they were heartbroken to hear of some of the women who had been close to the end of their pregnancies at the time they went off on study leave.

Three of the babies had not survived and, in one case, the mother and infant died, leaving six motherless children behind. This served to renew Letty's and Juliette's determination to fight for safer maternity care for women, when they were eventually practicing medicine in Edinburgh.

There were tears of joy and sadness when they said a final goodbye to the St Vincent de Paul organisers and clients.

Graduations were to be held in the Royal College of Physicians on Saturday the 1st of August. They had all agreed that it was too protracted a journey to expect their families to travel to Dublin for the ceremony, and had all written home and told them not to come for something that would probably last no more than an hour.

Instead they suggested a celebration when they returned to Edinburgh, possibly in the Assembly Rooms in George Street. That way the families and friends of the women could be there to celebrate with them. On consideration, their families had agreed that this was a much better idea and something more people would be able to attend.

Graduation day arrived and they were all up early and breakfasted by nine o'clock, ready to go and collect their graduation gowns and mortar boards from a hire shop near Kildare Street, where the college was situated.

"I don't think black does anything for me," complained Jessica, looking at her reflection in the full-length mirror. The dress code for the graduation was a black skirt and white blouse, with an optional black jacket.

"You look well," said Letty, but privately agreeing that black was not Jessica's colour, but she would never say that. Despite that, she did look well.

"It's alright for you Letty," Jessica replied, "you suit any colour with your lovely blonde hair and blue eyes."

The others joined them and, together, they managed to persuade Jessica that she looked radiant, she was just having pre-graduation jitters.

There was great hilarity in the hire shop, as they put on their gowns and mortarboards. "I hope a strong gust of wind doesn't blow this off my head, or I'll be chasing it all over the Quays and miss everything," said Emmeline as they left the shop and headed for the college.

They were still laughing and chattering away like magpies when they approached the college steps, and their progress was slowed by two people standing in the middle of the pavement. They were about to go around them when a voice said, "Aren't you going to say "hello" ladies?"

They stopped talking and looked up, stunned into silence by surprise. Letty was the first to speak, "Charles, what a wonderful surprise!" Then she looked at his companion and exclaimed, "Dr Cunningham, how lovely to see you too!" Everyone was laughing and saying how delighted they were at their unexpected appearance.

"It's good to see you ladies too and looking well in your academic robes," replied Wilf Cunningham. "We wouldn't have missed your graduation for the world!"

Letty looked past them both, half expecting others to be with them, but it was just Charles and Wilf.

Charles said, "You didn't think I was going to miss my sister's graduation, did you, despite your directive?"

"But it's such a long journey," said Marion.

Dr Cunningham replied, "Charles and I thought we'd earned a place at your graduation ceremony, what with me tutoring you and Charles finding this college for you." They all laughed and went up the steps into the graduation hall.

As each member of the *Edinburgh Six* was called by name to go up and receive her degree parchment, Charles and Wilf felt quite emotional and clapped harder than anyone else.

Afterwards they all went out to lunch and, although they

were invited, Charles and Wilf declined the offer of tickets for the Graduation Ball that night.

"We're taking the boat back to Liverpool tonight," said Charles. "We can't be away from work any longer, but perhaps you can show us around Dublin this afternoon and have an early supper with us before then."

"Rather," said Jessica, "we'd be delighted to, wouldn't we ladies?" She looked at her five companions and they all echoed, "Absolutely!"

Later, after supper, they all said their goodbyes before the men hailed a cab to take them to Kingstown for the overnight ferry.

"Tell Mater and Pater we'll be arriving at the Waverley at five o'clock on Tuesday week," said Letty. "We can't come before then as we have to pack everything up and vacate the house. We have made reservations for the ferry and trains and we'll be spending Monday night in Liverpool."

"I will," said Charles, "now off you all go and get ready for your well-earned ball!"

THE GRADUATION BALL was a great success. Everyone was in high spirits, especially the six new Edinburgh doctors and they celebrated getting their degrees with champagne and dancing.

36

THE RETURN OF THE EDINBURGH SIX
11TH AUGUST 1891

The women were tired after their lengthy journey, but not too tired to be excited at the prospect of being home and whatever the future held for them.

When they stepped down from the train on Platform 1, it was to a brass band playing "For he's a jolly good fellow", except, in their case, it was "she". The welcome home was even more of an occasion then their send-off in 1887.

There was a banner held high by their suffragist friends with: "Congratulations to our new lady doctors!" and each woman's name had been embroidered on it in beautiful gold and green threads.

There were reporters from the *Scotsman* and the *Edinburgh Evening News*, along with photographers. Someone had tipped them off that the *Edinburgh Six* were coming home with their medical degrees. The following day's editions had a photograph of the women with the headline, "Edinburgh welcomes home its six new women doctors", with a short article congratulating them on their success.

It quoted Dr Letitia Frobisher who said, "We could not have achieved this without the generosity and support of the people of Edinburgh. We owe a debt of gratitude and we will endeavour to repay you by offering our services to both the men and the women of this city. We shall be seeking positions in hospitals or medical practices, once we have settled back into life in Edinburgh."

Letty's parents had invited Charles and Louisa to Lauder Road that evening, to have supper and to welcome Letty home. Louisa, who hadn't seen her friend since the beginning of the year, hugged her with tears of joy wetting her cheeks. "Oh Letty," she said, "I am so proud of you. We knew you would do it. Congratulations my dear!" She hugged her again and added, "We have a special graduation gift for you, don't we Charles?"

"We do indeed," replied Charles, smiling from ear to ear, and he handed Letty a little jewellery box tied with a red ribbon.

"What can it be?" Letty asked, noting that it came from Laing's in George Street, one of Edinburgh's finest jewellers.

"Open it and see," said Louisa.

Letty opened the box and gasped, "Oh my goodness!" she exclaimed, "it's absolutely beautiful." It was a solid silver fob watch with a pearlised pale blue face and silver hour, minute and second hands. It had a short silver strap and pin. She hugged Louisa and Charles and pinned it to her dress. "Look Mother and Father," she said excitedly, "isn't it beautiful and so practical?"

Her mother looked at it and, then with a puzzled look on her face, she replied, "It is beautiful Letty, but the face is upside down dear." She looked at Charles wondering whether he had been sold a useless watch.

Letty, Louisa and Charles looked at her concerned expression and laughed. Letty put her out of her discomfiture right away, she said, "Only to other people. Mother, see, when I lift it to look at it, the watch face is the right way up for me," and she demonstrated it for her.

Her mother laughed with relief and, also a little embarrassment. "Oh dear," she said, "how silly of me!"

Her father said, "We also have a graduation gift for you Letty," and he reached behind an armchair and brought out a Gladstone bag in soft black Italian leather. It had "Dr L Frobisher" in gold lettering.

"Oh my goodness!" she exclaimed for the second time in five minutes, "my first medical bag." She stroked the soft leather and then opened it to look inside. "Oh!" she said, with delight, as she took out the new stethoscope, "now all I need is a practice to work in."

Louisa and Charles exchanged excited looks and Charles said, "You never know what's around the corner sister dear, I'm sure you and your fellow lady medics will be in much demand."

Letty looked at him questioningly, but "Anyone for another sherry?" was all he would say.

A FEW DAYS LATER, on Saturday evening, Letty and her five friends went to the special graduation celebration for them in the Assembly Rooms in George Street.

This had been organised by Letty and Louisa's mothers, along with the committee of the Edinburgh Women's Suffrage Association. Everyone who had helped with the Bazaar Ball, four years previously, were there also. They were all extremely proud of their members, who were a wonderful example of what women were capable of.

It was another glittering affair with the women in beautiful ball gowns and their jewellery sparkling in the candlelight. The evening was to begin with a light champagne supper, followed by dancing.

Charles had been asked to give a speech after the supper, to congratulate the six guests of honour on their success. The six women were seated at the head table, along with close family members.

"First of all," began Charles, "on behalf of everyone here, I want to congratulate you ladies on attaining your medical degrees, your registration and your licences to practice. Your determination and courage, in the face of the many obstacles put in your way, is truly admirable. This is especially so, as you had to travel to another country of the Kingdom, when the university in your own city rejected you, despite achieving the highest marks in the matriculation examination." He looked along the table and smiled at the six women. He continued, "Everyone here is exceedingly proud of you and I, for one, hold you in high esteem. Welcome to the medical profession! I know you will all do well in your medical careers, perhaps someone might join me in Paediatrics?"

Then he traised his glass, "To the Edinburgh Six!" Everyone got to their feet and echoed, "To the Edinburgh Six!"

Charles concluded his speech by saying, "The dancing is about to commence and I hope you all enjoy the remainder of your evening."

The orchestra struck up the first dance, which was a waltz, and couples moved eagerly onto the dance floor. The guests of honour were never without a dance partner all evening.

Dr Cunningham danced with Letty several times and after a particularly energetic polka, he asked her to step out of the hall and into an adjoining lounge. Curious as to why, she followed him out and they sat in the comfortable chairs in a quiet corner of the room.

"Miss Frobisher," he said "Charles did indeed speak for us all when he praised you and your friends."

"Thank you Dr Cunningham," Louisa replied with a smile.

"Please Miss er... Dr Frobisher, call me Wilf."

"I shall Wilf," she said, liking the sound of it, "if you call me Letty."

He smiled at her, a trifle nervous, and said, "Letty, I have a proposition for you, this is something I've been thinking about for some time." He paused, unsure how to proceed, then he took a deep breath and continued, "My practice is growing and I intend taking on a partner and I wondered whether you would like to come into partnership with me?"

Letty was so surprised, she hadn't expected this and she momentarily lost her voice. She said, "That is very good of you Dr .. er Wilf, but I had thought I would specialise in women's health, after working at the Rotunda in Dublin."

"Yes, well I was about to propose that you would look after my female patients, those that want you to that is, and I think most would, if not all." He cursed himself for babbling like a teenager. "Women's health would be your specialism, so, would you like to come into the practice with me Letty?"

As she listened to Wilf talk, she realised that this was a heaven-sent opportunity and she replied, "Yes, I would like to come into partnership with you Wilf, yes please." She was smiling from ear to ear.

"Oh I am so glad. Would you be ready to start on the 1st of September? Would that give you enough time to settle back in and rest from your travels?"

"The 1st of September is perfect Wilf," and she put out her hand to shake on the contract.

She was silent for a few moments in thought, then she asked, "Did Charles know you were going to offer me a partnership?"

Wilf had the decency to look sheepish as he replied, "Yes, he did actually. I approached him and asked him if he thought it was something you might be interested in."

Letty laughed, "I thought my brother had something up his sleeve the other night, when he and Louisa came to supper, but he wouldn't be drawn."

"Shall we go and tell the others the good news?"

"Absolutely." she replied.

37

IN CONCLUSION

Rose continued to meet with Louisa weekly for a further six months and as she talked through her experiences with Louisa, she became more confident and her self esteem increased immensely. The positive encouragement, without judging, that she received from Louisa greatly helped her to believe that she wasn't a bad person, that she wasn't to blame, and that what had happened to her at the Gideon Club in Royal Terrace, had been forced on her. She really did know that she had been an innocent child who had been coerced by depraved and ruthless men.

Towards the end of the six months, Rose was able to make her own way to Edinburgh by train from Dalmeny, near South Queensferry.

It was during her final meeting that Louisa told her about Maggie and that she had been employed as a housemaid in her home for some time.

"Maggie knows nothing about these meetings," she assured Rose, "and if you would like to, you may come and visit her on her next day off."

Rose's face lit up in surprise and she said, "Ah often

wondered over the years what had become o' Maggie and Lizzie. Maggie wis that good tae me, so she wis Mrs Frobisher and Ah wid love tae visit her."

"Maggie lives in as she has no home or family to go to, so you may come to our house to see her. Shall I arrange it for her next day off? I'm sure she'll be delighted to see you again," she asked Rose.

"Oh yes please," she replied.

Rose and Maggie became firm friends and Rose began to really enjoy life for the first time since she was a child. She also felt ready to look for work outside her home near Cramond and when Louisa heard this from the talkative Maggie, she recommended her to her mother-in-law, who was looking for a housemaid. Rose went into service with the Lauder Road Frobishers, where she was appreciated for her hard-working attitude and where she was treated well. Her friendship with Maggie continued throughout their lives.

OF THE *EDINBURGH SIX*, Marion and Victoria had applied for medical positions at the London Women's Hospital and had been successful. So the two who had been close friends for so long, went off to London on the next stage of their lives.

The hospital had been founded by the well-known doctor and suffragist, Elizabeth Garret Anderson, and was almost exclusively staffed by women.

JULIETTE RETURNED to Dublin to work in the Rotunda Maternity Hospital, where she received specialised training in Obstetrics and Gynaecology and eventually became a consultant in the field.

JESSICA JOINED the medical staff of *The Hospice* in George Square, ironically, close to the Edinburgh Medical School in Teviot Place, where they were attacked by medical students in 1887.

The Hospice was a seven-bed facility for the poor women of Edinburgh and had been founded by Dr Elsie Inglis. Dr Inglis had also established, alongside the hospice, a centre for specialist training in gynaecology and midwifery.

LETTY HAD GONE into partnership with Dr Cunningham and worked, predominantly. with female patients, although she would also see men and provide cover for Wilf when he was away. They shared out-of-hours or emergency call-outs and this arrangement guaranteed each of them a whole weekend off every fortnight.

Letty wanted to increase her knowledge and skills in women's medicine, especially in obstetrics and gynaecology and she and Wilf often discussed the dearth of resources in this field. To that end, she enrolled in the training centre attached to the Hospice and trained under the auspices of Dr Inglis one day a week.

EMMELINE SUCCESSFULLY APPLIED for a position in a large medical practice in Stockbridge. Her credentials, as one of the *Edinburgh Six,* stood her in good stead with the progressive, pro-female doctors and pro-suffrage all-male practice. Lady Moncrieff was delighted since that was where she consulted her physician. On hearing of Emmeline's appointment, she immediately registered to be added to her patient list.

LOUISA REMAINED SERVING on the Edinburgh School Board, challenging policies that she felt were unfair, or where resources were being allocated to more affluent areas when they were needed more in the poorer schools.

CHARLES TRIED, unsuccessfully, to interest the Hospital Board in psychiatric services for children, but he was determined not to give up on the idea.

EVANGELINE CONTINUED to be a happy and bright child. She would soon be old enough to be enrolled in her mother's alma mater, the Edinburgh Ladies College in Queen Street, where she would be a bright and popular pupil, like her mother had been.

The End

TO BE CONTINUED.... You can catch up on the lives of the characters from this book and meet new ones in Book 2 of *The Frobisher Family Saga*, coming next.

AFTERWORD

The main theme of this book is how the Victorian patriarchal system prevented women from having the same rights as men, in a male-dominated society where women were meant to stay in their own *sphere* i.e. the home, and were not allowed to enter, or even think of entering, *men's sphere* i.e. society, politics, certain professions and, generally, the world outside the home.

Men argued, without any evidence, that it was a "fact" that women were physically and intellectually inferior to men, and should be protected from the outside world. They propounded the belief that it was "against nature", "God" and "the social order" to allow women to participate in society on equal terms; that it was "God's plan" that they should stay within their sphere.

We must ask the questions: was this protection or control? And, how far have we actually come since then, in terms of equality between the sexes?

THE FRANCHISE AND WOMEN PARLIAMENTARIANS

It is one hundred and three years since women were

granted the parliamentary franchise and in the 2019 General election, only 34% of the MP's elected were women. In P.M. Johnson's cabinet reshuffle in September 2021, out of the 30 members only 8 were women. That is 26.6%, which is even less than the low overall percentage of women in Parliament.

By contrast, in the Scottish Parliamentary election earlier this year, 2021, a record 129 MSP's elected were women, which is 45%. It is still less than equal numbers, but it's a step in the right direction. In Wales this year 43% of elected members were women which is a slight increase from 2016, but much less than in the early years of devolution. The figure for the Northern Irish Assembly comprised a poor 21% of women members.

Clearly, this is a long way from gender equality in the British parliamentary system. Yet we owe a great deal to the women who fought to have the vote, even as far back as 1832, when the first petition to give women the vote was submitted to parliament. That is almost 200 years ago and I can't help feeling that progress, in this area, is moving at a snail's pace.

There were many Victorian suffragists who also campaigned for equal rights in other spheres, such as higher education and equal pay. They were not naive enough to think that gaining the franchise would solve all the inequalities between men and women. They knew that there would be many other battles ahead. But, I wonder, did they know women would still be fighting against such issues well over a hundred years later?

NOTE ON "MAGDALENES"

At the time period this book is set in, this was a pejorative term used to describe "promiscuous" women. It was used by Professor Laycock, of the Faculty of Medicine at Edinburgh University, to describe the *Edinburgh Seven* who wanted to be doctors and who were attacked at Surgeon's Hall in 1870. He suggested that they might be "basely inclined" or might [even] be "Magdalenes". The *Times* wondered why he wasn't equally concerned about male students. Of course there was no male equivalent due to blatant double standards in Victorian Society and this still exists in society today. (Where is the male equivalent of "slut"?)

The implication is that these women were "fallen women", like Mary Magdalene in the Bible, who is generally thought to have been a prostitute. The term was applied to young women in Ireland in the 20th century, who found themselves pregnant, and were sent to the notorious "Magdalene Laundries".

MODERN DAY ATTITUDES AND MISOGYNY

In recent times, we have seen increasingly high incidences of misogyny, to the extent that women, especially those who have a public profile, are receiving vast amounts of hate mail and threats to their lives, from men who have never even met them or know them. It is not just women in the public eye that are targeted with hate, but women going about their day to day business are being accosted in the street by men using foul language and sometimes physical violence towards them.

Sadly, even some politicians display misogynistic attitudes and use sexist language. In the UK at the moment, there is reluctance to class misogyny as a hate crime, although, in Scotland, a working group is currently looking into whether their Hate Crime law could be amended to make misogyny an aggravating factor, and a decision will be made early in the new Year. (2022)

The other worrying factor in the increase in misogynistic attitudes and behaviour, I believe, is the plethora of online violent pornography. Research has demonstrated a clear link between men watching violent pornography and men perpetrating sexual violence against women.

FEMICIDE

Since the high-profile rape and murder of Sarah Everard in March 2021, according to a report in the Guardian, at least 81 women have been killed by men to date. (8th October 2021.) This rape and murder is significant because it was committed by a serving policeman, whose job it was to protect the public. *(End Femicide Campaign)*

The *Femicide Census* (2018) revealed that half of UK women killed by men, die at the hands of their partner or ex-partner. Worryingly, these figures have been increasing over recent years and there surely must be a correlation between this and a society that appears to tolerate this amount of violence against women.

I believe the lack of specific laws and measures to eradicate this behaviour is the result of the gender composition in the UK Parliament. There appears to be insufficient urgency or political will to change how women are treated.

Kay Race, October 2021

ACKNOWLEDGMENTS

I would like to thank my husband, Keith Race, for the time and commitment he has contributed, in editing the manuscript and making this a better book to read. His thoroughness and patience is very much appreciated.

My warmest thanks go to my friends and family who have encouraged and supported me on this journey, including Nell and Trish in Connecticut, Sam Thomas, Marie Robertson, Anne McKay and Jim Divine. Your enthusiasm is heart-warming and I appreciate it very much.

ABOUT THE AUTHOR

Kay Race was born in Edinburgh in 1954 and was educated at St Thomas Aquinas Senior Secondary School. She left at age 16 to work in the civil service. A decade later, as a young mother, she graduated from Edinburgh University with a Joint Honours Degree in Sociology and Social Policy. Her undergraduate dissertation led her on to postgraduate research into child abuse and neglect in 19th century Edinburgh.

Kay worked for many years as a psychotherapist and counsellor, specialising in working with survivors of childhood sexual abuse and domestic violence. Retired now, she lives in rural Northumberland with her husband and two sight hounds, Poppet the whippet and rescued greyhound, Bertie.

Visit her website at: www.creaking-chair-books.com

Follow her on Twitter.com@KayRace2

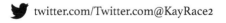 twitter.com/Twitter.com@KayRace2

ALSO BY KAY RACE

Trapped in the Dark Decade

November 2018

Book 1 in the Dark Edinburgh Series

Dark Past, Secret Present

October 2020

Book 2 in the Dark Edinburgh Series

Dark Hearts, Enlightened Souls

May 2021

Book 3 in the Dark Edinburgh Series

Published by

Creaking Chair Books

If you would like to be kept up to date with new releases from Kay Race, please complete an email contact form on her website:

www.creaking-chair-books.com

GLOSSARY OF SCOTS WORDS

- aboot - about
- Ah - I (first person singular)
- ain - own
- an' - and
- awfy - awful or awfully
- bairn - child
- cannae - can't
- couldnae - couldn't
- dae - do
- daein' - doing
- didnae - didn't
- dinnae - don't
- disnae - doesn't
- doon - down
- efter - after
- feart - afraid
- flair - floor
- gie' - give
- gie'n - given

Glossary of Scots Words

- gon - going
- hadnae - hadn't
- hame - home
- havnae - haven't
- hen - term of endearment (female)
- hissel - himself
- hoose - house
- intae - into
- isnae - isn't
- ken - know
- lassie - girl
- mair - more
- nae - no
- o' - of
- oot - out
- sae - so
- tae - to or too
- tellt - told
- thae - those
- wee - little, small
- wi' - with
- wid - would
- widnae - wouldn't
- wis - was
- wisnae - wasn't
- ye - you
- yer - your, you're

MISCELLANEOUS NOTES

TIMELINE OF CHILD PROTECTION IN EDINBURGH

1877 - Edinburgh and Leith Children's Aid and Refuge founded by Emma Stirling

1887 - name changed to the Edinburgh Society for the Prevention of Cruelty to Children when it joined another organisation, in Edinburgh, that had set up to do the same work. Around this time, Emma Stirling withdrew her considerable funding, to date, and concentrated on her work in Nova Scotia, where she had taken a number of children as emigrants.

1889 - the Edinburgh Society amalgamated with the Glasgow Society for the Prevention of Cruelty to Children to become the Scottish National Society for the Prevention of Cruelty to Children (SNSPCC).

1889 - First Act of Parliament, for the Prevention of Cruelty to Children, passed. Also called "The Children's Charter".

1894 - Prevention of Cruelty to Children Act - included "mental cruelty".

1921 - SNSPCC received the Royal Charter to become the RSSPCC

1995 - Charity changed its name to "Children First" to reflect its new role and services.

POLICE FUND

I anticipated this scheme by 3 years, in order to fit in with the timeline in my story. The Police Aided Clothing Fund was actually established in 1892 and was instituted by the Lord Provost and the Chief Constable of Edinburgh to *alleviate the suffering of necessitous children* and, in exceptional cases, adults. Its main priority was, and still is, to provide school shoes and warm jackets for school-age children.

FREE SCHOOL MEALS

It was argued in the 19th century that, if the government has made attendance at school compulsory, then it ought to provide free school meals. A report published in 1889 indicated that over 50,000 pupils, in London alone, were attending school *in want of food*.

Other studies, such as those undertaken by Booth in London and Rowntree in York, found that almost a third of the population were living in poverty. Interestingly, the large proportion of men rejected as recruits for the Boer War, was on the grounds of malnourishment.

Louis'a's success in getting the Edinburgh School Board to agree to provide free school meals for the poorest children in Edinburgh's schools, is purely fiction, since The Education (Provision of Meals) Act did not become law until 1906.

The Act, which was the result of a private members's bill by a Labour MP, set out the provision of free school meals for children in most need and was means tested. However, it did not compel Local Authorities to provide these meals, so provision varied throughout the country. Despite its limitations, the Act led to an increase in the number of children being fed a healthy meal while at school.

Children going without food is not only a problem of the late 19th and early 20th centuries. According to the *Child Poverty Action Group* (CPAG), there were 4.3 million children living in poverty in the UK in 2019-20.

Many children were going hungry during the pandemic lockdown in the spring of 2020, with the government refusing to provide needy school children with free meals while schools were closed. The government changed its mind (U-turn) after ongoing campaigns by Manchester United footballer, Marcus Rashford, and again, later in the year, was persuaded by his campaign to provide meals for school children during the Christmas holidays.

Made in the USA
Columbia, SC
12 November 2021